W9-CRX-057

From the Case Files of Shelby Woo

THE CRIME: A Mars rock is stolen from a touring exhibition at the space museum. The same day half a million dollars' worth of gems disappears!

THE QUESTION: Is Shelby's classmate Tom guilty as charged—or is someone trying to frame him? Too many people have the motive—and the means.

THE SUSPECTS: *Morgan Kane*—the museum's owner has plenty to hide, and good reason to want Tom out of the way.
Dave Pitt—Kane's assistant caught Tom snooping in the files. Is there something *he* wants to conceal?
Tom Rivers—Shelby's classmate has a secret—and so far he's paying way too high a price for concealing it.
The Phantom—the infamous thief is in town. No one knows who he is—or when he'll strike again. He has already left his calling card for the police.
Melanie Burgess—Kane's brilliant scientific adviser labels all his exhibits and knows where all the bodies are buried. Has the arrogant Dr. Burgess committed the perfect crime?

COMPLICATIONS: Shelby has her eye on the clues—but the pieces of the puzzle aren't falling into place as Tom lands in jail with no prospect of getting out!

For orders other than by individual consumers, Pocket Books grants a discount on the purchase of **10 or more** copies of single titles for special markets or premium use. For further details, please write to the Vice-President of Special Markets, Pocket Books, 1633 Broadway, New York, NY 10019-6785, 8th Floor.

For information on how individual consumers can place orders, please write to Mail Order Department, Simon & Schuster Inc., 200 Old Tappan Road, Old Tappan, NJ 07675.

HOT ROCK

JOHN PEEL

A
MINSTREL®
BOOK

Published by POCKET BOOKS
New York   London   Toronto   Sydney   Tokyo   Singapore

The sale of this book without its cover is unauthorized. If you purchased this book without a cover, you should be aware that it was reported to the publisher as "unsold and destroyed." Neither the author nor the publisher has received payment for the sale of this "stripped book."

This book is a work of fiction. Names, characters, places and incidents are products of the author's imagination or are used fictitiously. Any resemblance to actual events or locales or persons, living or dead, is entirely coincidental.

A MINSTREL PAPERBACK *Original*

A Minstrel Book published by
POCKET BOOKS, a division of Simon & Schuster Inc.
1230 Avenue of the Americas, New York, NY 10020

Copyright © 1997 by Viacom International Inc. All rights reserved. Based on the Nickelodeon series entitled "The Mystery Files of Shelby Woo"

All rights reserved, including the right to reproduce this book or portions thereof in any form whatsoever. For information address Pocket Books, 1230 Avenue of the Americas, New York, NY 10020

ISBN: 0-671-01154-5

First Minstrel Books printing September 1997

10 9 8 7 6 5 4 3 2 1

NICKELODEON, The Mystery Files of Shelby Woo and all related titles, logos and characters are trademarks of Viacom International Inc.

A MINSTREL BOOK and colophon are registered trademarks of Simon & Schuster Inc.

Cover photography by Jeffery Salter and Tom Hurst

Printed in the U.S.A.

This is for Jason Quick

HOT ROCK

Chapter
1

You've all heard that old saying that some people will steal anything that's not nailed down? Well, I always used to think that was just plain stupid. I mean, there are lots of things people wouldn't take even if you gave them away! But then I was involved in this really strange case where the stolen object was a rock. A rock! Can you believe it? I couldn't, at first, but then it turned out that this rock wasn't just something you might dig up from your garden. It was a pretty special rock after all.

"I don't know, guys," Noah Allen said, studying the door in front of them. "This looks *way* too much like homework to me. And school doesn't even start up for another week."

"Some days," Cindi Ornette answered, "I wonder why we let you tag along. Try and think positive. This is going to look great on our résumés. Right, Shelby?"

Shelby grinned, knowing that both of her best friends were actually happy about going along with her on this mission. They both also liked to argue. "I suppose it's a bit of both," she said diplomatically. "If you look at it one way, it *is* like homework. But it's also great career experience. Plus," she finished, "it's going to be a lot of fun."

"A *museum?*" asked Noah, incredulously. "These are the lamest places on earth."

"Only if you let them be," argued Cindi. "You can learn a lot from them if you just show a little enthusiasm."

"I think my enthusiasm just died," Noah replied. "A museum . . ." He made it sound like the sentence of doom.

"Don't be so negative," Shelby told him, clutching her tape recorder and checking for the third time that the battery levels were fine. "If we do a good write-up on this for the school paper, we'll get extra credit in English. Besides, it's not just a museum—it's a *space museum*. And even you have to admit that space isn't boring."

Noah shrugged. "It didn't use to be," he agreed. "But it's getting kind of routine these days." He studied the door again. Above the large entrance hung a new sign: Kane's Traveling Space Museum.

The exhibition wasn't due to open to the public until tomorrow. It was housed in an old department store building that had gone out of business a year or so back and been vacant since. Then, just a month ago, the whole site had become a flurry of activity. Workmen had started to clean the place, then several large container trucks had arrived and been unloaded. The work obviously wasn't quite finished, because there were still several workmen hurrying around the site, carrying things back and forth from the remaining container truck.

"Honestly," Cindi said with a sigh, "you are far too preoccupied with the wrong things. Space exploration is a fascinating, ongoing event that should thrill you."

"So sue me," Noah suggested. "I'd rather cover a rock concert any day."

3

"Well, there aren't any on right now," Shelby pointed out. "The only new thing in town right now is this." She gestured at the museum and turned to Cindi. "You've got plenty of film?"

Cindi was the photography buff of the trio. She and Noah both worked after school in a photo shop, and Cindi was really good at taking as well as developing film. "That's the fourth time you've asked me," Cindi complained. "And, just like the last three times, the answer's *yes*, okay?"

"Right." Shelby gave her friends a grin. "Then let's get on with it."

She marched up to the door, and had to duck aside as a workman hurried out, heading back toward the truck. Before the door could swing shut, Shelby held it, and the three of them walked inside.

Despite the activity, Shelby could see that the exhibit was very close to being finished. It should be fine for its scheduled opening tomorrow. It took up the whole floor of the old store. The walls were hung with huge blow-up photos that depicted scenes of space exploration—one of Earth from the moon, another of a nebula, and several of the space shuttle in action. These hid the bare walls. The rest of the space was taken up with exhibit cases and display stands. These were all gleaming white, topped with see-through covers.

Shelby gazed around, interested. There were space suits, both whole and in parts. There were models, some of them several feet long, of various spacecraft. There were pieces of rockets and other space debris. She could see several satellites that looked like they were either real or else full-scale reproductions. There were more giant photos, with descriptive cards. Telescopes and other instruments littered the room. Hanging from the ceiling were huge representations of the planets orbiting a central sun. It was all very impressive. Cindi should be able to get plenty of good pictures to illustrate the article.

"Hey, you kids!" yelled a man, heading toward them and waving his arms. He was in his forties, Shelby saw, and rather overweight. He had on a bright yellow Hawaiian shirt, open to expose part of a hairy chest. A gold chain hung around his neck, swaying as he stormed across to them. His brown hair was thinning, and swept back into a ponytail. "Come on, clear out. The exhibit doesn't open till tomorrow. You want to see it, you buy tickets. Okay?"

"Uh, hi," Shelby said, swallowing slightly under the barrage of his aggression. "I'm Shelby Woo, and there is Noah Allen and Cindi Ornette. We're from the high school paper. I talked to Mr. Kane about doing a piece on the exhibit."

"Oh, yeah, right." The man stuck out his hand. "I'm Morgan Kane, kids. Sorry about the misunderstanding there. We get a lot of kids who hang around, getting in the way, wherever we go. It can get dangerous, so we don't usually allow it."

That's not what you said a moment ago, Shelby thought. He'd been more concerned about their getting a free peek and not buying a ticket. But, then, he was a businessman, after all. And his income was bound to be his main concern. "Thanks for agreeing to talk to us, then," she replied.

"No problem. Any publicity is good publicity, and all that stuff." Kane gestured about the room. "As you can see, we're not quite ready for the opening yet, but we should be by the day's end. It looks like a madhouse, but we're getting there. So, what do you want to know?"

Taking the tape recorder out, Shelby started it

going, and held it toward him. "Could you tell us a little bit about your museum, Mr. Kane?" she asked.

"Sure thing," he agreed, grinning affably. "I was always a bit of a space nut. I remember the day Neil Armstrong first set foot on the moon. I was in school then. And I remember thinking that this was the greatest event in human history, bar none. And I realized that what I wanted to do was to be a part of it somehow. I couldn't be an astronaut—all that technical stuff just confuses me—but I realized that I could do something better. I could bring the space age to the average person. So I created my traveling museum.

"You see," he went on, obviously warming to his favorite subject—himself—"there's plenty of space stuff in museums all over the world, but the drawback to that is that you have to get up and go there to see it. I mean, the National Air and Space Museum in Washington, D.C., has a great collection—if you can get there. My idea was to take the stuff to the public. Go where they go. We've done fifteen cities so far this year, from Seattle to Chicago and Des Moines. And in those places, there's not a lot of other spots you can go to and see authentic space stuff. That's why my show—my *museum*—is so popular."

"Thank you," Shelby said, glad to get a word in finally. "You certainly seem to have a lot of exhibits. Maybe you could show us some of your favorites and tell us a little about them."

"Is it okay for me to take photos?" asked Cindi, holding up her camera. "To illustrate the interview."

"Sure, kid, sure," agreed Kane. "Maybe you should get a couple of me with some of the exhibits," he suggested. He led the way over to one of the space suits. This was an old one, looking a little worn. It was on a mannequin, and Kane put his arm around its shoulder. Cindi obligingly snapped a couple of pictures of him.

"This is a neat item," he said. "Alan Shepard's original suit. He was the first American to orbit the earth, in nineteen sixty-one."

"And you've got his suit?" Shelby was impressed. "That's terrific."

"Just the start of our treasures," Kane assured her, winking. "Come and see some of the real gems here." He led them over to what looked like a rock inside a glass case. "What do you think of this?"

8

Noah snorted. "It's a stone," he said. "Big deal."

Kane wasn't offended. His grin widened. "You're right," he replied. "It *is* a stone. And it *is* a big deal. This isn't just the average, everyday common or garden rock you'd find digging in your garden. It comes from the planet Mars."

"Oh, wow." Shelby looked at the rock with a little more appreciation. It certainly looked average enough—just a dark rock with faint pockmarks all over it.

"This was formed millions of years ago on the planet Mars," Kane explained. "It was thrown into space by volcanic activity and ended up here on Earth as a meteorite. Cool, hey?" He grinned. "You probably heard that some scientists think that there's evidence of ancient life in these rocks from Mars. There aren't too many of them on Earth, and that's what makes this little beauty such a treasure."

"You wouldn't think it was worth anything to look at it," Noah commented.

"It's one of the most valuable things in my collection," Kane said proudly. He pointed to the glass. "Bulletproof glass. And there's a very sophisticated alarm system in that case to deter any potential burglars. Top-of-the-line computerized stuff. Spared no expense." Then he glanced over Shelby's shoulder and scowled. "Is *she* with you?"

Shelby turned around and followed his gaze. A pretty blond girl was standing nervously just inside the door. "No, she isn't," she admitted. "But I know her from school. Her name's Brittany Cox."

Brittany shares some classes with me. Her parents are wealthy lawyers, and she's always wearing great clothes and accessories. But she's a bit standoffish, and doesn't make friends easily. She hangs around with a couple of other girls I don't know too well.

"I don't care if she's the Queen of England," Kane snapped. "Hey, you!" he yelled across the room. "No freebies. Beat it!"

Brittany went red. "Uh, no, I'm just here to wait—" she started to explain.

"Then wait someplace else," Kane said, glowering at her. "This isn't a school bus stop. Out."

Before Brittany could make a move, though, there was another interruption, this time from the far end of the exhibition room. A door slammed open, and a large, burly looking man marched out, one hand around a young black man's arm.

"Boss!" the newcomer called. "I caught this kid snooping in the office. He's a thief!"

Chapter
2

At the word *thief*, Shelby's interest perked up. But she couldn't help staring at the upset youngster. She knew him from school, too. "That's Tom Rivers!" she exclaimed.

Tom's a nice kid, but a bit odd. He's constantly going places with people and then begging off and vanishing. We're talking way unreliable here. Still, he's a hard worker and likable, so people excuse him for some of his odder behavior.

"I know who it is," growled Kane angrily, turning his attention to the boy. "I hired him to help, after all. What do you mean by repaying me like this?"

Tom seemed more angry than guilty, Shelby realized. "I wasn't *stealing* anything," he replied sullenly. "I was just . . ." He let his voice trail away.

The second man growled in his throat. "He was going through the filing cabinets, boss," he said. "Probably checking to see what was worth stealing."

"Well, I'm glad you caught him, Dave," Kane replied, barely controlling his anger. To Tom, he added, "I don't care *what* you were doing. You knew that room's off limits to you. You were just hired to help set up and label these exhibits. Well, you're out of a job now. You're lucky I don't hand you over to the police. Now, get out of here." He jerked his hand toward the door.

"Well, I'll *tell* you what I was doing," Tom snapped back angrily. "It's these exhibits of yours that started me off. A lot of them are out-and-out fakes! I was checking in your files for proof of that. I've told you this before."

"Yes, you did," agreed Kane. He eyed Shelby and her friends. "And I told you then you were wrong. I have certificates of authenticity for every one of them."

"Most of which are signed by Dr. Burgess," Tom retorted. "And you pay her salary, so how reliable are they?"

Kane was obviously having a hard time keeping his temper. And he was only managing that, Shelby realized, because she and her friends were there. This was turning into a potentially fascinating story! Kane winced as Cindi took a picture of him and Tom.

"That's slander," Kane finally snarled. "I could sue you for that. You heard me—out of here, now. Or I will call the police." Looking for another target, he glowered at Brittany. "You, too. I don't care why you're here—clear out."

"I'm going," Tom snapped. "But you haven't heard the last about this, Mr. Kane. I'm going to get even. You just wait and see." He grabbed his pack from beside the door and stormed out. With an anxious, hurt look on her face, Brittany followed him out.

Kane swallowed, and took a deep breath. As he let it out, he managed to calm down a little. "Sorry you had to witness that," he said, trying to recover the situation. "He came highly recommended. Who's to know he's just a would-be thief?"

"I know him from class," Noah said firmly. "He's no thief. He's a real hard worker."

"You can never be sure," Kane commented vaguely. "I trusted him, and look what happened."

Shelby felt a mental itch growing. "What about his allegations?" she asked, holding up the tape recorder to show that she was still working as a reporter. "Are your exhibits faked?"

"Certainly not!" Kane exclaimed. "Look, I've spent a lot of money on this venture, and I've hunted down items from all over the world. Why would I possibly resort to fakes? As I said earlier, all of my exhibits are looked over by Dr. Burgess. Why don't you come and speak to her? She'll tell you the same thing." He turned to the other man. "Dave, where is she?"

Dave gestured toward the back. "In her office, working. As always."

"Thanks." Kane led the trio across the hall. "That's my right-hand man, Dave Pitt," he explained. "Dave looks after a lot of things. He designs the exhibits, for example, and makes sure they're packaged safely when we hit the road again. He's very good at his job, and he's always on the ball."

"And this Dr. Burgess?" Shelby prompted. "What about her?"

"She used to work for NASA," Kane explained. "Until cutbacks a few years ago. That's why she knows the space stuff so well. She's really into science, all the stuff I don't really know." They passed through a door at the back into a short corridor. Several doors led off this. "Offices, kitchen, bathrooms," Kane said vaguely. He gestured toward one of the open doors. "This is her room." He rapped on the door, and peered inside. "Not here. Well, she'll be back in a minute, I should think. Come on in."

Shelby slid into the room. It held a large desk with a computer and all the trimmings—scanner, laser printer, modem, fax, and a stack of CD-ROMs. There were books, papers, and files also on the desk. Two large filing cabinets, both with more files and books on them, stood under the small window. There was an open briefcase on the floor, and a closed laptop computer.

"Here, I'll show you some of the stuff she does," Kane offered. He went to the computer and started banging at the keys. "Uh, just a second. I'll get back to the menu, I know—"

"Kane!" an anguished voice said from the doorway. "Don't touch another button, you idiot!" Shelby was brushed aside as a tall woman rushed inside and shoved Kane away from the keyboard. "You almost wrecked the file I was working on!" she snapped, tapping feverishly at the keys. "I've told you before—stay off my computer. You don't have a clue about these things."

Kane scowled. "You seem to forget who's paying for that thing," he growled.

The woman sighed, and straightened up. She was tall and slim, with a thatch of honey blond hair. This was obviously Dr. Burgess. "Sorry, Morgan," she apologized. "It's just that you were on the verge of wrecking my figures, and I got a little upset."

"No harm done," he said, generously. Then he waved vaguely at Shelby, Cindi, and Noah. "These kids are from the school paper, covering the opening. Good publicity, and all that."

"Oh." The woman stuck out her hand at Shelby. "I'm Melanie Burgess. Nice to meet you."

"Shelby Woo," Shelby replied. Dr. Burgess

seemed very pleasant and genuine, unlike the volatile Kane. Shelby returned the cheerful smile. "We just had an . . . incident outside that Mr. Kane said you might be able to clear up."

"Dave caught the Rivers kid snooping in the office," Kane explained. "Looking for something to steal, but he claimed he was looking for proof that our stuff here is all faked."

Dr. Burgess sighed. "That again?" She shook her head and then smiled at Shelby. "Tom's a nice enough kid, but he seems . . . well, a trifle *obsessive*. He decided that a couple of our exhibits couldn't be real because he'd read something somewhere that made him think they weren't. I told him he was wrong, but he refuses to give up on it." She glanced at Kane. "And if he's been trying to rob the office, then I think it proves he's not exactly totally balanced." She gave Shelby a sympathetic smile. "Look, if you're his friends, I think the best thing you can do for him is to convince him to get counseling. He really needs it." Then she sighed again. "And what I really need is to get back to work, I'm afraid." She gestured at her computer screen. "Lots of boring figures to finish before we're ready to open tomorrow."

Shelby nodded sympathetically. She knew from her own computer work at the police department how much paperwork there could be to get done some days. "Thanks for your help, though, Doctor."

"You're welcome." Dr. Burgess gave Kane a quick look. "I know it wouldn't occur to you, Morgan, but how about giving these three kids free passes to the exhibition? They seem like nice people, and if they like it, I'm sure they'll spread the good word and help attendance."

Kane scowled at the suggestion. Shelby realized it was because he was thinking of the fact that he'd lose three paying admissions. And he was obviously balancing this against the thought of the good publicity. Then he managed a smile, which looked almost painful. "Sure," he agreed. "Great idea. Tell you what . . ." He fished in his jacket pocket and pulled out three cards. "You can have these. Unlimited passes. Be sure and tell everyone about the museum, okay? And give us a good write-up in the paper." He handed the cards out to Shelby, Cindi, and Noah.

"We'll do our best," promised Shelby honestly. "I can definitely say that we'll be giving you a good write-up. This place seems fascinating."

"Terrific. Now, I don't want to rush you, but like the lady said, the show opens tomorrow, and we've got lots to do, so . . ." Kane ushered them to the door, and then across the exhibition floor to the exit. "See you around, kids."

Noah raised an eyebrow as the door shut behind him. "Wow. Talk about being eager to get rid of us." He eyed his pass, and then slipped it into his pocket. "Somehow I don't think I'm going to get a lot of use out of this."

"Me, either," agreed Cindi. "I mean, it's a nice exhibition and very well laid out. But it's not something I'm likely to keep on visiting." She turned to Shelby. "I know that look, Shelby. What's going on?"

Shelby grinned at her friends, totally caught up in her own thoughts. "Tom Rivers claims that some of the exhibits are fakes," she murmured. "Can't you see the story in that? If we can *prove* that Kane's passing off fakes to the public . . ."

"Earth to Shelby," Noah replied, waving a hand in front of his friend's face. "In case you forgot, both Kane and Dr. Burgess said Tom was mistaken. And that he was trying to steal from them."

"Come on," Shelby replied. "You know Tom from school. Does he strike you as a thief?"

"No," agreed Noah. "But I don't know him *that* well. Just in the odd class now and then. Plus seeing him at a couple of dances and parties. It's hardly enough for me to be sure of anything about him. He doesn't hang around with us at all."

Cindi frowned. "Well, I have to admit, I kind of like the guy. He's quiet, and studies hard. His hero is Ronald McNair—you know, one of the astronauts who died in the *Challenger* explosion? Tom always said he wanted to be an astronaut, too, and he's really a whiz at science." She chewed at her lip thoughtfully. "You know, Shelby, you may have a point. I mean, I can see him taking a job at this museum to be close to the space stuff he loves. But why would he jeopardize his whole life by trying to steal from the place?"

"Especially when there are so many people around," Shelby pointed out. "He was almost bound to get caught." She shook her head. "No, something here doesn't quite add up, and I think we should check it out."

Noah sighed. "I *knew* you were going to say that," he complained. "Look, Shelby, not *everything* in life is a crime to be solved. This could just be exactly what it looks like, you know."

"Maybe," agreed Shelby cheerfully. "But wouldn't you like to *know?* Look, guys, I'd better get started on writing this up. And tomorrow morning I have to work. But how about we get together for lunch, and then see if we can contact Tom and talk with him? Get his side of the story? At the very least, it'll add some spice to our piece for the school paper."

"I knew it," complained Noah, rolling his eyes. "The slightest scent of a mystery, and you're off. Trust me on this one, Shelby. There's *nothing* to this story. You wait and see. We won't even hear about this space museum again."

I was *certain* that Noah was completely wrong here. I could feel that I was on the verge of . . . well, *something*. I just wasn't sure what, but something was about to happen.

Chapter
3

Detective Hineline was one of the smartest people that Shelby had ever met. He was also one of the busiest. His desk always looked like a hurricane had camped there for a few weeks. No matter how hard she tried, Shelby could never quite get it clean. As soon as she filed away all of his folders, checked and discarded all of his stick-on notes, the cycle would begin again.

She was filing away folders when he came rushing into his office and slammed down into his chair. He began pawing through his desk.

"You've been cleaning up on me again," he

complained, head down. "I can never find any-thing when you do that to me."

"It's my job, Detective," she reminded him cheerfully. "What are you looking for? Maybe I can help you find it." She crossed to the desk and bent to see.

He batted her gently but firmly away. "You've done enough already, tidying up," he growled. "And it has to be when I *have* to be places." He started searching through the large central drawer.

Shelby's ears prickled at this one. "Trouble?" she asked eagerly. "A case?"

"Trouble, yes. A case, yes." He looked up for a moment from his search. "And, *no*, you can't tag along."

"If you tell me what you're looking for," Shelby said, "I can probably get it for you. What's the case about?"

"My car keys," Hineline answered. "The case is about a gem robbery, over at Kemp's."

I've heard of the place. It was the most upscale store in town. Diamonds the size of eggs, so they said, and other rare and valuable gems. The sort of place where Brittany Cox's parents bought presents. I ached to be in on this one.

"Detective, *please*," she begged.

"No way, Shelby," he replied. "That's my job, not yours. Keys. Do you know where they are?" Before she could answer, the phone on his desk rang. He scooped it up. "Hineline. I don't want to be interrupted when . . . Oh, all right. Put him on." With a long-suffering expression, he cradled the phone between his shoulder and ear, and kept on searching through his desk drawers. "Morgan Kane? Yeah, Detective Hineline here. Look, I'm kind of busy right now and . . ." His voice trailed off. "Somebody stole your *what*?" He almost dropped the phone and snatched it out of the air, and held it back to his ear. "Your rock? Look, I'm sure it's real important to you, but I have a serious . . ." He paused to listen again. He tried to interrupt the voice several times, and then finally managed: "Look, Mr. Kane, we have a major crime on our hands right now. I can't come myself. But I'll send over an officer to check out your story, and I promise you, we'll do everything we can to get your Martian rock back. Fine, have a nice day." He put the phone down.

"Morgan Kane?" she echoed. "Someone stole his Mars rock?"

"Yeah. You never know what some people will steal. Crazy." Then he caught himself. "You know the guy?"

"I interviewed him yesterday for the school newspaper," Shelby explained.

"Oh." Hineline lost interest. "Ramirez!" he yelled, and then turned back to Shelby. "Keys," he repeated.

"Oh, yes." Shelby smiled, and pointed to the coat stand in the corner of the office. "I put them in your coat pocket. You always wear your coat when you go out on a case."

"Coat pocket?" Hineline shook his head. "Crazy place to put them. I'd never have looked there." He crossed to the stand and pulled on his coat, feeling in his pocket and then hefting out his car keys.

At that moment, Ramirez arrived. She was a young detective sergeant—lean, with short-cut dark hair and a glint of humor in her eyes. "You wanted me, sir?" she asked.

"Yes, I do." Hineline bent over his desk, and

ripped off the notes he'd made when he'd been talking on the phone. "Get over to this space museum place. There's been some kind of odd robbery. Check it out, and call in whatever help you need. But be realistic. I'm going to need most of the force on this Kemp's heist."

"Got you, sir," Ramirez agreed, studying the note.

"Detective," Shelby said, eagerly.

"I told you, you can't come, Shelby," Hineline said.

"You said I couldn't go with *you*," Shelby replied. "But I've been to the space museum. I know Mr. Kane. And we took photos of the place yesterday. I might be able to help the sergeant."

Hineline paused, obviously about to say *no* again, and then looked thoughtful. "You know the place? And you took pictures?"

"Yes," Shelby said eagerly, trying to project her most professional expression. "I can help here, honestly!"

Hineline considered it and then turned to Sergeant Ramirez. "It's up to you. What do you think?"

The sergeant looked at Shelby, and couldn't restrain a smile at what she saw on Shelby's face.

"Well, she does know police procedure, Detective," Ramirez replied. "And as long as she doesn't get in the way—"

"I won't, I promise!" Shelby said.

Hineline rolled his eyes. "Anything to get out of cleaning my office," he said. "Okay, you can go. *But*"—he held up a hand to restrain her enthusiasm—"you do *exactly* what the sergeant tells you. No poking around on your own for clues, nothing. You're there just to help out *as needed*. Got that really clear?"

"Absolutely, Detective," Shelby promised, hardly able to contain her enthusiasm. She was being allowed along on a case! And she could watch and listen to a police detective and learn from her. Way cool!

Hineline sighed, and headed for the door. "Keep an eye on her, Ramirez," he advised over his shoulder. "Otherwise she'll be into everything." He shook his head as he left.

Sergeant Ramirez grinned and then winked at Shelby. She stuck out a hand. "I'm Judy," she offered. "You're Shelby Woo, right? Everyone talks about your grandfather. He must be a really nice guy."

"Yes, he is," Shelby agreed, falling into step

beside Judy Ramirez. "Thank you so much for letting me come with you. I *promise* to be quiet and stay out of the way."

The sergeant laughed. "When I saw your eyes, I couldn't say no," she admitted. "You remind me of myself at your age. I wanted to be a cop so badly." They were out in the lot now, and Ramirez led the way to her car. "So, what can you tell me about this place?"

On the drive across town, Shelby filled the sergeant in on what she knew. When she had finished, Ramirez nodded.

"So the rock is actually pretty valuable, then? That makes it more interesting. I was starting to think it was just some sort of juvenile prank."

That sparked something in my memory. Tom Rivers . . . When he had been thrown out of the museum the previous day, he'd promised to get his revenge. Could he have stolen the rock, and this was his idea of revenge?

"So," Shelby asked, trying to sound casual, "what's this big case that's got Detective Hineline so worked up?"

"I don't know much myself," Ramirez said.

"Just that somebody broke into Kemp Jewelers overnight and stole about half a million dollars' worth of gemstones. The odd thing is that the shop has one of the most top-notch security systems in the country, and it didn't even make a squeak."

"That sounds like a great case," Shelby said, wistfully. "Uh, not that this one doesn't, of course," she said hastily, in case her companion got the wrong idea.

"Of course." Ramirez nodded. "Well, here we are." She pulled her car into the parking lot, and the two of them headed for the space museum. There was a small line of people waiting by the door, and Shelby saw Kane talking animatedly with them. He glanced up as they moved toward the crowd, and broke away from the line.

"Thank heavens you're here!" he exclaimed. "I can't let anyone in until you've looked around, and I'm losing money." He looked in anguish at the impatient line of people. "Could you, you know, hurry this up a bit?"

"I'll do my best," Ramirez promised. "But I can't give you any guarantees."

Kane nodded impatiently. "We'll get you inside fast and—" He broke off as he stared at

Shelby in puzzlement. "You're a bit young to be a cop, aren't you? And don't you look kind of familiar?"

"I'm not a policewoman," Shelby replied. "I just help out there. And you saw me yesterday, when I interviewed you."

"Yeah, right," Kane agreed. He rapped on the door, which was opened by Dave Pitt. He let the three of them in and then closed it behind them. "So," Kane continued, hurrying them across the floor, "how long do you think this'll take?"

"Hard to tell until I examine the scene," Ramirez said. She pulled her notepad from her uniform pocket. "Then you can tell me what happened."

Shelby whistled as she saw the damage. The previous day, the Martian rock had been seated in a cradle under the glass display case. Now it looked as if someone had taken an ax to the case. The glass was shattered and scattered all over the floor. The cradle was broken, and the wood and metal display stand had been hacked several times. Whoever had broken into the case had done a terrific job of destruction.

Ramirez stood back several feet and looked

at it. "Has anyone touched anything there this morning?" she asked.

"No," Kane answered. "I came in first, and saw it like that. I immediately called the police. Dave arrived a few minutes later, and we've stayed clear of it since."

Nodding, Ramirez started to walk about the case. "I'm going to have to get a fingerprint team in here to examine this case," she decided. "I doubt the thief was stupid enough to attack it without gloves on, but you never know." She shook her head. "Whoever it was certainly did a number on that. You're going to have to replace it."

"The second time in two weeks," complained Kane. He sounded really mad about it.

"Really?" asked Shelby, curious. "It was broken into before?"

"I'll ask the questions, Shelby," Ramirez said gently. Shelby nodded guiltily, forgetting she was supposed to stay quiet until spoken to. Ramirez raised an eyebrow at Kane. "Care to explain that remark?"

Kane shrugged. "No, it wasn't broken into before. On our last stop in Chicago, Dave accidentally broke the case by hitting it with a crowbar when we were dismantling some exhibits. I had to have it replaced then. The stupid thing seems to be always causing me trouble."

"Clumsy of him," Ramirez remarked.

"I docked his pay for it," Kane answered. "I don't believe in subsidizing stupidity. Look, can we get on with the important stuff?"

Ramirez gave him a cold stare. "I think I'm best equipped to judge what's important, sir," she said politely. "Now, I assume everything was fine when you left for the night?"

"Yes," Kane snapped. "You think I'd have left it like that? Dave and I both left together at nine o'clock last night. Everything looked okay. Then, at nine this morning—that."

"I see." Ramirez was taking notes as she talked. "And you went where after closing up?"

"To my bed-and-breakfast," Kane answered. "The Easterly Breeze. Why? What difference does it make?"

The Easterly Breeze is the bed-and-breakfast place that my grandfather bought after he retired. I help him out there when I can, doing all sorts of little jobs around the place. I hadn't realized Kane was there, but it did make sense. It was affordable, and Kane hated spending money. And it meant I might be able to find out some more about the man.

"I don't know yet," Ramirez replied. "I just have to consider everything." She turned to Pitt. "And how about you?"

"Well, I'm also staying there," he replied, shrugging. "But I was hungry, so I went for a bite to eat first. At Chez Luis. You need the address?"

"No," Ramirez replied. "I know where that is. Nice restaurant."

"Maybe," Pitt growled. "But they sure serve some odd food. I'm not likely to go back there again."

Ramirez nodded, and studied the scene again. Then she turned to Shelby. "Anything about this look different from yesterday?" she asked. "Aside from the obvious?"

Shelby stared hard at the broken stand. "Just one thing I don't understand," she admitted. "When I interviewed you yesterday," she said to Kane, "you said that the case had a really sophisticated alarm on it. How come it didn't go off?"

3 4

Kane managed to look embarrassed. "I could sue the stupid alarm company," he answered. "Not a peep out of the thing. I checked it when I came in, but it was still set. However, the alarm to this one case had been turned off."

"Turned off?" Ramirez and Shelby echoed together, both surprised. Shelby hastily clamped her mouth shut, and Ramirez asked: "How could that be done? Don't you need the code to do that?"

"Yes, you do," Kane answered. "Someone put in the correct code and turned off the alarm to the case. Then they broke into it and stole the rock."

"Then it had to be someone who knew the code who stole the rock," Ramirez said. "Unless we're dealing with a burglar who can crack such codes."

Kane went red. "Are you saying *I* did it?"

"Not necessarily you," Ramirez answered. "But how many people knew the code for the alarm?"

"Three," Kane snapped. "Myself, Dave, and Dr. Burgess."

"Dr. Burgess?" asked the policewoman.

"She's my scientific adviser," Kane replied. He

glanced at his watch. "She should be here in about fifteen minutes."

"Uh, there is one other person who could have known," Pitt added, slightly hesitantly. "I mean, I don't *know* he knows it, but . . ."

Ramirez cocked her head to one side. "Would you mind explaining that?" she asked, patiently.

"Well, yesterday I caught this kid we hired going through some files in Mr. Kane's office. One of them was the alarm file. He could quite easily have seen the combination there, because Mr. Kane always writes it down." He looked apologetic. "He sometimes forgets it, you see."

"Rivers!" Kane exclaimed. "That's right! That boy was trying to steal from me." He turned to Shelby. "You were here, weren't you? The brat wasn't grateful when I just threw him out instead of having him arrested. And he promised he'd get even with me." Kane swept his hand out toward the shattered case. "And this is what he did!"

Shelby stared at the wreckage in shock. Kane was right—things certainly did look pretty bleak for Tom Rivers.

Chapter
4

Ramirez didn't seem to be overly impressed with Kane's accusation, though. "Do you have his home address?" she asked. "I'd better have a talk with him. *After* I've finished taking your statements."

Kane scowled at her. "Why are you wasting time here? Just go and arrest him! That's your job!"

Ramirez shook her head. "That's *not* my job," she said carefully. "My job is to arrest the guilty person. So far, you've only leveled accusations at the boy. I'm going to need some evidence that he's involved before we can even talk about arresting anyone. I need to speak to Dr. Burgess next. You said she'll be here any time, so that's fine. Meanwhile, I'm going to call for the fingerprint squad to come and collect all the evidence they can. I don't want anyone touching anything till they arrive." She looked at Shelby. "Make sure nobody does, okay?" She headed out for her car to call in her request.

Kane and Pitt obviously thought that Tom Rivers was behind the theft. And I'd heard him promise to get his revenge on Kane. But would he go this far just to pay back a boss he claimed was cheating? People sometimes did some funny things when they thought they were in the right. And, also . . . Tom was a space nut. Maybe he'd wanted the Martian rock for himself for some reason? Such a thing would be too expensive for him to buy, after all. And why would anyone else want to steal it? It wasn't like jewels, or stolen coins, or anything—the kind of stuff that there was a ready market for. Who'd want to buy a stolen Mars rock?

When Ramirez came back, she was accompanied by Dr. Burgess. The scientist looked tired and flustered. She stared at the broken display case and shook her head. "Vandals," she complained. "Sheer, wanton vandalism. There was absolutely no need to break that case if whoever stole the rock bypassed the alarm, as you said."

"Right." Ramirez had her notepad out again. "And you weren't here when Mr. Kane and Mr. Pitt locked up last night?"

"No," the scientist answered. "I left about half an hour earlier." She hefted her laptop computer. "I took this to my hotel and worked on the figures all night."

"And did anyone at your hotel see you? Where is it, incidentally?"

Dr. Burgess shrugged. "The Bay View," she replied. "The night manager gave me my key, but I didn't see anyone after that. I worked until almost one in the morning on the figures, all alone."

"I see." Ramirez closed her notepad and then turned to Kane. "The crew will be here in about fifteen minutes." She eyed the wreckage. "Once they've gone over that area and taken samples, you'll be able to open up shop."

"How long will that take?" Kane asked, irritated. "I'm losing money!"

"Probably less than an hour," Ramirez informed him.

"An *hour?*" Kane threw his hands up. "I'm being robbed twice in one day!" He turned to Pitt. "Well, go on out there and start calming the patrons down. Tell them they can watch the police at work, or something. Maybe they'll find being at a crime scene exciting." A sparkle came into his eyes. "Hey, maybe we can get some free publicity from all of this. I'm going to call the local papers." Rubbing his hands, he strode off to his office.

"All broken up about this robbery, isn't he?" Ramirez remarked.

Dr. Burgess smiled. "He's a businessman, first and foremost," she explained. "His whole life is dedicated to making money. You can't blame him for seeing the financial angle in this. Which reminds me, I'd better get onto the insurance company. Kane has a good policy, and if the rock isn't recovered, we'll need to file a claim fast."

"One last thing," Ramirez said quickly. "I understand you used to work for NASA." She waved her hand around the room. "Isn't this a bit of a comedown for you?"

For once Dr. Burgess showed a little anger. "Yes," she agreed, trying to stay cool. "It is. But two years ago, I was laid off. They kept plenty of the men, who were less capable than me, but let me go. My brilliant record meant nothing to them. This was all the work I could find that was still connected even vaguely to space." She snorted and stared at Shelby. "It's a man's world," she said. "With all of our advances, we women are still second-class citizens." She scowled, and then hurried off.

Shelby raised an eyebrow. "She seems a little bit harsh," she commented.

"Some people get like that," Ramirez replied. "Maybe she's right, and she was laid off simply because she's a woman. But maybe her attitude had something to do with it. She might come across as a bit arrogant."

They waited until the forensics team arrived. Ramirez went over to hand over control of the crime scene to the lead officer. Shelby stayed closer to the scene of the crime, knowing she'd only be intruding otherwise.

I couldn't help wondering if Ramirez was right. Was this an inside job? We had four suspects so far. Tom Rivers *might* have done it, if he'd really known the override code for the alarm. But did he? Then the other three definitely knew the code, but why would they rob the exhibition? And why take only the Martian rock?

Ramirez beckoned her across the room, and Shelby hurried to join her, her mind still trying to make sense of what they'd learned so far.

"I've got to head off and get some more statements," she said. "You'd better come with me. I can't leave you here with the squad, I'm afraid. It's too early for me to let you go home yet."

"That's fine," Shelby said hastily. As long as she was still involved, even minimally, she was happy. "I'm glad to stick with you."

"Fine." They went out to her car and Ramirez checked her notes. "The closest place is Chez Luis," she decided. "But they don't open until lunch, so maybe we'd better check some of the others first." She grinned at Shelby. "How about starting with your grandfather?"

It didn't take them long to reach the Easterly

Breeze. Grandpa Mike was at the front desk, as usual. He was restocking the rack of local travel brochures, and smiled as he saw Shelby and Ramirez come in.

"She's not in trouble, I hope," he said, with a faint smile. "Or is she just getting in the way?"

"Neither," the sergeant said, smiling back. "She's helping me with my case. Maybe you can do the same. I understand that Morgan Kane and Dave Pitt are both staying here?"

"That's right." Grandpa Mike nodded. "Is there a problem?"

"Someone broke into their museum last night," Ramirez replied. "It looks like an inside job. Can you tell me when they both came in last night? And if either of them went out again afterward?"

Grandpa Mike thought for a moment. "Mr. Kane arrived about half past nine," he said. "He had some sort of take-out with him. He went straight to his room. I was on duty here until almost midnight, and didn't see him come down again."

"Could he have left without your seeing him?"

"It's always possible," Shelby's grandfather agreed. "But his room is on the second floor, so he'd have to have climbed out of his window and shimmied down the drainpipe or something. And Mr. Kane doesn't look like the sort of man who shimmies anywhere."

Ramirez laughed. "No, he doesn't," she agreed. "And Pitt?"

"He came in about eleven-thirty," Grandpa Mike said. "He mentioned he'd been to a restaurant and hadn't been very happy there."

"That's what he told me, too," Ramirez agreed. "And he stayed in after that?"

"I believe so, yes." Grandpa Mike's eyes sparkled as he regarded his granddaughter. "You look as though you're having fun."

"I am!" Shelby said. She turned to the sergeant. "Where next?"

"The Bay View," Ramirez answered. "Let's check up on Dr. Burgess's alibi."

This was another bed-and-breakfast, just a mile down the same road. The hotel manager there thought for a moment and then nodded. "She came in about nine last night," the woman replied. "Went straight to her room. I didn't see her again until she left this morning. She keeps to herself a lot. Quiet sort."

"Could she have left and returned without your noticing it?" asked Ramirez.

"I suppose so," agreed the woman. "Her room's down the hall there, and has a patio. If she wanted to, I suppose she could have gone out and returned that way."

As they left, Ramirez checked her watch. "I think the restaurant should be opening about now," she said. "Let's try them next." It was a short drive back. Chez Luis wasn't actually open to the public, but the manager let them in when Ramirez rapped on the door.

"The waiters from last night?" he said, in reply to Ramirez's question. "Well, two of them are here now. If you're lucky, the one you want will be here. If not, I suppose I can give you the addresses of the others."

The second man was the right one. Ramirez described Pitt to him, and the man nodded emphatically. "Table four last night," he said. He pointed to a table by the window. "Right there. He was here just after nine and left forty-five minutes later."

"How can you be so sure?" asked Ramirez.

"Do you remember all your customers that well?"

"No," the waiter admitted. "But I remember *him* very well. He ordered the special last night—red snapper in a delicate pepper sauce. He complained that it was too salty, and demanded that I take it back and have the chef redo it. He was . . ." The man looked faintly embarrassed. "Let's say he was less than polite about the whole matter. He's not someone I'd be likely to forget."

"Thanks," the sergeant said. As she and Shelby headed for the car, she shook her head. "Pitt sounds like a really fussy character. He must have really kicked up a stink last night." She glanced at her notebook. "Well, that leaves just Tom Rivers to talk to. You know him?"

"He goes to my school," Shelby replied. "I know him a little."

"Then it's probably a good thing you're with me," Ramirez said. "This way, it'll be less intimidating for him. I don't want him to think that he's the chief suspect."

"You mean he isn't?" asked Shelby, interested.

"There is no chief suspect yet," Ramirez replied with a laugh. "Shelby, I've only just started investigating. It's a grave mistake to start suspecting anyone too soon in a case. You might overlook clues that point to other people if you do. At the moment, I've got lots of suspects."

"Right." Shelby was lost in her thoughts until they arrived at the Rivers house. It was a pleasant little place, tidy and cheery. Mrs. Rivers answered the door when the sergeant knocked.

She looked worried when Ramirez asked to speak to Tom. "Is he in some sort of trouble?" she asked.

"I don't know, ma'am," the police woman answered honestly. "I'm investigating a theft, but there's nothing to worry about yet. You can stay with me while I talk to your son if you like, and if it'll make him feel more comfortable."

Mrs. Rivers nodded, and then went to fetch Tom. He emerged from his room a moment later, a scowl on his face.

"So, Kane did file a complaint about me after all," he said.

"No," Ramirez replied. "But this does have something to do with the events of yesterday at the space museum. Can you just tell me where you were last night?"

"Last night?" Tom looked definitely confused. "I was out . . . with some friends."

"For how long?" persisted Ramirez. "And can you give me the names and addresses of those friends?"

Scowling again, Tom asked her: "What's this about? Why are you checking up on me? What's going on?"

The sergeant sighed. "The museum was apparently broken into last night, and a rock was stolen. It had to have happened after nine o'clock, so I need to know where you were. You were with friends, you say? Then all you have to do is to give me their names and addresses, and I'll be able to confirm your story."

Tom's face looked as if it had been set in stone. "No," he said coldly. "I'm not telling you anything. I've got nothing to say to you at all."

"Tom!" his mother exclaimed. "What's gotten into you? Why won't you tell her where you were, and who you were with?"

Tom shook his head. "I know my rights. I don't have to tell her anything. And I won't."

He turned his back on them and marched back to his room.

Stunned, Shelby watched him go. She realized that Tom had virtually admitted his guilt—he'd offered no explanation for himself at all.

Had he committed the robbery after all?

Chapter
5

As they drove back to the precinct, Shelby asked Ramirez, "Why do you think Tom wouldn't answer your questions?"

"I don't know quite what to think yet," the sergeant answered, "except that he's being very foolish. He's quite right that I can't *make* him talk—but he has to realize how guilty his refusal to speak to me makes him look."

Tom had looked surprised when he'd heard about the robbery. Maybe it was just an act? But if he was innocent, then why wouldn't he talk? Why would anyone steal a Martian rock?

Grandpa had told me that there were three reasons for any criminal behavior: greed, revenge, or insanity. The third was the hardest to figure out, but also the rarest. People generally committed crimes because someone had something they wanted, or because they wanted revenge on someone for some reason.

Stealing the Mars rock for greed didn't make a lot of sense. It wasn't the sort of thing you could sell inconspicuously. Maybe a collector might steal it. But revenge . . . Tom *did* have a grudge against Kane, so he had a motive. But would he have stolen the rock just to annoy his former boss? If it was an inside job, as Ramirez suspected, that meant there were three other people who could have done it: Kane himself, Pitt, or Dr. Burgess.

Why would Kane steal his own rock? Besides, he seemed very annoyed about the smashed case. If he'd stolen the rock, then why had he smashed the case as well? Just to make the crime look more authentic? Anyway, he said that he'd left the museum with Pitt, and Grandpa had confirmed he must have gone almost straight back to the Easterly Breeze.

Maybe he had slipped out again later, but there was no proof of that.

Pitt? Kane seemed to treat him like a slave, but Pitt didn't seem to mind the treatment very much. At any rate, he showed no resentment. Could he have stolen the rock? If so, why and when? He'd have had to have gone back to the museum sometime in the night to do it. And why would he do it? To annoy his boss? Or maybe some other reason?

Dr. Burgess? Well, she had left early, and the rock was there when she'd left. And she'd arrived late this morning, after the loss had been discovered. Of course, she, too, could have slipped back in the night to steal the rock—but, again, *why* would she do it?

What really puzzled me was the shattered case. If the theft was an inside job, then the thief must have known that there was no need to break the case once the alarm was off. So why had he?

Then maybe Sergeant Ramirez was wrong, and it *wasn't* an inside job. But who else would have been able to disable the alarm?

Back at the station, Shelby headed for Detective Hineline. As interested as she was in her case—well, that's how she considered it!—she wanted to hear about his. A big jewel heist was simply too fascinating to ignore. But before she could ask him anything, he marched over to Ramirez's desk. Shelby tagged along, ears perked.

"I've pulled the forensics team out of the museum," he told her. "They've got all the samples they need, and I need them to check out Kemp's." He ran a hand through his hair. "That's a mess."

"Tough case?" Ramirez asked sympathetically.

"One of the sort I hate," Hineline answered. "Somebody turned off the building's alarm. They knew the password, it seems. It looks like an inside job. Except . . ."

"Except what?" asked Ramirez. Shelby could hardly contain her excitement.

Hineline pulled an evidence bag out of his pocket. It was sealed and initialed, and inside it was a simple business card. "This was there."

Ramirez glanced at the bag and her eyes widened. "The Phantom!"

Unable to restrain her curiosity anymore, Shelby asked, "Who's the Phantom?"

"Don't we wish we knew?" Hineline growled.

Then, realizing who had asked the question, he turned around to her. "I told you to stay out of the way."

"I will," she assured him, still trying to sneak a glimpse at the card. "Please, Detective, won't you tell me what that card is all about?"

"You don't need to know," Hineline said. "But the Phantom is the name of some supercrook that strikes all over the country. Whoever it is targets jewelry stores, really upscale shops, that kind of place. Always manages to turn off the alarm, and always leaves his calling card. He likes to mock the police." He held up the bag, and Shelby could see that the card simply read: Compliments of the Phantom.

"Going to analyze the card, chief?" asked Ramirez.

"Yeah. But I already know what the answers are going to be. There won't be any fingerprints, and it's been run off a common brand laser printer, the sort that almost every computer buff has." He sighed. "And if this job *was* done by the Phantom, there won't be any other clues at the scene of the crime, either."

Shelby frowned. *"If?"* she repeated. "But doesn't that card prove that it was?"

"No, it doesn't," Hineline answered. "It proves only that someone wants us to think the Phantom did the job. Maybe it *was* the Phantom. But maybe it was an inside job, and whoever did the theft is trying to sidetrack us. Don't jump to conclusions." He turned back to Ramirez. "How are you doing?" he asked her.

Ramirez told him. When she finished, Hineline nodded. "Sounds to me like you're right," he agreed. "It certainly looks like an inside job. Nobody in their right mind would steal a lump of rock otherwise."

"It's pretty valuable, Detective," Shelby said. "They sell for tens of thousands of dollars."

"But who'd buy one like that?" Hineline frowned. "Only another museum, and they'd *have* to know it was stolen." He shook his head. "No, either this is going to be offered back to Kane—for a finder's fee, of course—or else it was stolen for revenge. And this Rivers kid looks very suspicious. Well, Ramirez, it's your case. What do you want to do next?"

The sergeant smiled gently. "I'd like to ask Mr. Rivers to come to the station for questioning," she replied. "Maybe if we talk to him here, he'll realize what serious trouble he might be in if he doesn't give us some answers."

"Sounds like a smart move to me," Hineline said. "Go ahead and try it." He managed a small grin. "I'll even come in and bark at him a bit if you like. I feel pretty grouchy right now." He turned to Shelby. "Which reminds me—I really need some coffee and a doughnut. Brain food."

"Right away, Detective," Shelby said smartly. If she stayed on his good side, maybe he'd continue to allow her to work along with Ramirez. She fixed his coffee perfectly, and even found a sprinkle-topped doughnut for him, then hurried back to his desk with them. With a grunt, he took the coffee and then bit out a large piece of doughnut. "Anything else I can do, Detective?" she asked sweetly.

Hineline looked up. "Check the new reports," he told her. "And one more thing. Don't start thinking I've gone soft or anything, just because I let you go along with Ramirez this morning. It's not going to happen again."

Shelby couldn't keep the disappointment from her face and voice. "But, Detective," she exclaimed, "I was just starting to get into this case, and—"

"But *nothing,*" he snapped. "Shelby, this is official police business, not a Nancy Drew case, okay? Ramirez is a very competent officer, and it's *her* case, not yours. You're an intern, not a policewoman. So—stay out of this. I mean it."

Shelby sighed and forced herself to nod. "I understand," she said sadly. "I know I'm not a detective. But I want to be."

"I know that." His voice softened slightly. "And I'm sure you might well be, one day. *After* school, and *after* police academy, and *after* some experience on the force. Right now, stick to what you're supposed to do, okay? Learning to obey orders is just as important as solving mysteries if you really want to be a good detective."

Shelby nodded, and retreated to her computer. She began to call up the files she had to proofread and cross-reference. But as she worked, she couldn't get her mind off the Mars rock theft.

Shortly before Shelby had to get ready to leave, Tom Rivers arrived at the station with his mother. Mrs. Rivers looked scared for her son, and very worried. Tom looked worried, too, but there was also determination written on his face. Ramirez, trying to look reassuring, led them both to an interview room. Shelby continued her work, one eye on the clock, one on the room's door.

After about ten minutes, Detective Hineline went into the interview room. Shelby was due to leave in another five minutes, but she didn't want to go while Tom was still being interviewed. She wished she knew what was going on in there! As slowly as she could, Shelby started to pack her things away.

Just when she couldn't stretch it out any longer, Hineline popped out of the interview room. "Shelby! Get over here, now!"

Shelby dashed across the room eagerly. "Yes, Detective?"

Hineline jerked his thumb back over his shoulder. "You know this dope in here. Well, come and talk to him. Maybe *you* can get him to give us something more than his name, rank, and serial number. And remember, he isn't a suspect yet. We just want him to talk to us. He's only hurting himself by staying silent."

Shelby nodded, and followed him into the interview room. Ramirez, looking just as bothered as Mrs. Rivers, managed a wan smile of greeting. Hineline growled again, and gestured at the seated Tom. He looked scared, but adamant.

Hineline jerked his head at Ramirez. "We'll wait outside." The two officers left, closing the door behind them.

"Tom," Shelby said gently, "you must realize you could be in serious trouble here. They think you stole the Martian rock, and by not talking to them, you're only making them more convinced."

"I don't care," Tom said defiantly. "I didn't do it."

"Why won't you just tell them where you were, then?" Shelby asked reasonably. "They just want you to give them an explanation."

"I don't have to give them *anything*," Tom replied. "I know my rights."

"Rights?" Mrs. Rivers asked, her eyes brimming with tears. "Son, you've *got* to tell them. I couldn't bear it if they locked you up."

"They can't arrest me," Tom said, but there was uncertainty in his voice. "Mom, I didn't do it, honestly. They can't arrest me if I've done nothing."

Shelby realized he still didn't quite understand. "They can hold you on suspicion," she explained. "All they have to do is to convince a judge that they have enough evidence against you for that. And if you won't tell them where you were, that might be enough to swing it. They don't actually have to charge you with the crime to be able to hold you for a couple of days." She put as much concern into her voice as she could. "Tom, *please* tell them where you were. I'm on your side."

Tom shook his head, his jaw very tight. "No deal," he said stubbornly. "Let them lock me up, then, if that's what they want."

"They don't *want* it," Shelby told him, exasperated. "But you're not really leaving them any choice."

"Sorry," he said, folding his arms across his chest.

Shelby couldn't understand what was wrong with him. He didn't seem to realize what a jam he was in. But it was clear that she wasn't going to get any further than Detective Hineline or Sergeant Ramirez had. With a sympathetic glance at Mrs. Rivers, Shelby left the room. "It's no good," she told Hineline. "He refuses to talk at all."

Hineline let out a long sigh. "Then we'll have to hold on to him for a while. Ramirez, you'd better see about getting the kid a lawyer. Maybe that will make him wake up." Hineline rubbed his chin. "Shelby, you're leaving now. Would you mind offering to see Mrs. Rivers home? It's going to be tough on her, seeing her son locked up. I'm going to have to see about getting a search warrant, to have a look for the rock. Though if he *did* take it, he'd have to be dumber than a box of rocks to hide it in his house."

"No problem," Shelby answered. There was a tingle of excitement within her. Despite Hineline's earlier word, she still considered herself on the case. And now she had a unique opportunity. . . .

Chapter
6

One of the policemen drove Mrs. Rivers and Shelby back to the Rivers' house. Shelby saw the grieving mother to her door. She could see that Mrs. Rivers was very badly affected by what had happened.

"Mrs. Rivers," Shelby said gently, "you know I'm on Tom's side, don't you?"

"Yes, dear," she replied, patting Shelby's shoulder. "And I thank you for it."

"Could I ask a big favor of you, then? Would it be okay for me to take a look in Tom's room? Maybe I can find something—anything—that might tell us where he was last night, and why he won't talk."

Mrs. Rivers thought about it for a minute, and then slowly nodded. "I expect it'll be all right. Just don't disturb anything, please."

"I'll be very careful, I promise," Shelby answered. She'd have to be, because Sergeant Ramirez was likely to be the next person to look in it, and she didn't want the policewoman to know yet that she'd been there. If she was lucky, she might get some clue as to why Tom was acting so oddly.

His room was very neat and cheerful. Instead of posters of rock stars or TV celebrities in bikinis, he had space pictures all over the wall. Opposite the bed was one of astronaut Ronald McNair, and a sticker that said "Aim for the stars!" On shelves there were model kits of the space shuttle and earlier capsules. The bookcase was crammed with books on astronomy and space travel. It was very clear that Tom had a one-track mind about his future. But what I needed now was something about his past. A diary would be the best thing, if he kept one.

Shelby looked over his desk, which was as neat as the rest of the room. There was a computer, but he probably had password protection for it. Besides, she doubted he'd keep a diary on it. She started to search through the desk drawers. One had files of news and magazine clippings on space, which was of no help at all. Shelby realized that he was clearly something of a space expert. Maybe, then, his accusations about Kane faking some of the exhibits were right?

And then she hit pay dirt. The drawer stuck a little when she tried to push it back in. Something was catching, somewhere. She put her hand in the top of the drawer to see what, and discovered there were some papers stuck in the top. Excitedly, she pulled them out. Maybe they'd just been misplaced, but it looked to her as though they had been deliberately hidden.

She glanced at the top sheet and stiffened in shock.

"Dearest Tom," it began, and then went into a page of rather sickly sweet endearments. It was a love letter, with a large red heart drawn in at the bottom. And inside the heart, the name *Brittany*. She flicked through the pages, and discovered that there were eight letters, all from Brittany to Tom.

The only possible person it could be was Brittany Cox. She'd come to the museum the previous day to meet someone, she'd said. Of course, it had to have been Tom! That was why she'd been so shaken when Tom had been fired. The two of them had to be dating! Which meant that Tom had probably been out with Brittany last night. But, if so, why hadn't he simply said so? It didn't make any real sense.

Shelby carefully replaced the letters, and then went off to find Mrs. Rivers. "Does Tom have a girlfriend?"

"Tom?" Mrs. Rivers smiled thinly and shook her head. "He's too wrapped up in his schoolwork," she replied. "Since his father died a couple of years ago, Tom knows how important it is for him to go to college and get his degree. He won't let anything sidetrack him."

So she didn't know about the letters. . . . Well, it wasn't Shelby's place to rat on Tom right now. Maybe this was the reason Tom hadn't told about Brittany? Because he didn't want his mother to know? But surely that was less important than his freedom?

Shelby offered some more encouragement to

Mrs. Rivers before leaving and heading back to the police station. Her mind was in a whirl, and only one person could help to sort it out right now: she had to confront Tom with what she knew.

Detective Hineline had gone out again when she arrived back at the station, working on interviewing the staff at Kemp's. Ramirez was still there, though, and Shelby asked her if she could talk to Tom. "I have an idea," she said. "I think I may have found a clue as to where he was last night."

"Well, I suppose it won't hurt," the policewoman replied. "I'll bring him to the interview room, and you can talk with him there."

Shelby could barely restrain her excitement until she was alone with Tom. Then she stared hard at him. "Tom, I know where you were last night. You were on a date with Brittany Cox, weren't you?"

Tom looked at her in shock. He was obviously a terrible actor, because it was clear she'd caught him completely by surprise. "Uh, no," he denied.

"Tom, stop playing games," Shelby snapped. "I *know* you were. What I *don't* know is why you won't simply tell the police that. I'm sure Brittany would back up your story, and the police would let you go."

"It's no good," Tom insisted. "I can't do that."

"Why not?" Shelby persisted. "If you don't tell me, I'll have to tell the sergeant what I know, and they'll just ask Brittany anyway."

"No!" Tom said, in near panic. "Shelby, *please* don't involve Brittany. Promise me you won't!"

"I can't promise anything if you don't tell me the truth," Shelby answered. "Why is it so important to keep Brittany's name out of this?"

Tom seemed to collapse inwardly. "Okay," he said in a quiet voice. "I'll tell you. *Provided* you don't tell the police without my permission."

"All right." Shelby was certain that it wouldn't be too hard to convince him that he was wrong and should talk to Sergeant Ramirez.

"The problem is Brittany's parents."

"They don't like you?" guessed Shelby.

"They don't like *anybody* for their daughter," Tom said grimly. "Her parents are very rich, and—well, you know my family isn't. Since Dad died, Mom's barely been able to keep her head above water. That's why I took the part-time job, to earn some extra cash for us. The Coxes would think I'm just after Brittany for money if they knew about us. And, on top of that, they want her to become a lawyer so bad they can taste it. Both of her parents are corporate lawyers, and they decided that Brittany had better become one, too. That means lots of studying and applying herself. They've forbidden her to date because that would only be a distraction. She's only allowed to go out with her girlfriends, not guys."

Shelby was starting to get the picture. "And she's been ditching them to date you instead," she finished. "And if they knew, they'd throw the book at her."

"Yeah," Tom agreed. "A big, thick law book. She'd be grounded for the rest of her life, and they'd be *so* mad at her." He looked earnestly at Shelby. "I *can't* put her through that, I just can't. So I don't want her name mentioned at all in connection with this case. I didn't steal the rock. They can't possibly prove I did, so they're going to have to let me go sooner or later."

Shelby shook her head in wonder. Tom was willing to spend time in a jail cell to avoid getting Brittany Cox into trouble with her parents. He had to really like the girl, since she could clear him with just a few words. "Okay," she said, finally. "I won't tell the police, I promise. And I also promise that I'll do everything I can to prove that you're not the thief."

"Thanks, Shelby." Tom sighed with relief. "But how can you do that?"

"The only possible way," she replied confidently. "By catching the real thief."

He looked at her in amazement. "Can you do that?"

"Piece of cake," she promised him. Then honesty compelled her to add, "Once I figure out just *who* did take the rock, that is."

Later, she met with Cindi and Noah again when they both got off work. They all went for burgers at C.J.'s and a chat. Shelby filled them in on what had been happening—or as much as she could tell them. She didn't feel it would be right to mention about Tom and Brittany. Cindi had brought along prints of the photos she'd taken the previous day.

"If we examine them," she suggested, "maybe we'll see something suspicious."

"Maybe," agreed Shelby. They had started to go over them when Will arrived with their orders. As they shuffled pictures out of the way to clear spaces for their burgers and fries, Will caught sight of one of the pictures.

"Hey, I know that guy," he said, pointing to a shot Cindi had taken of Dave Pitt. "He's in here all the time."

"Really?" Shelby gave him a sympathetic look. "Poor you."

"Huh?" Will looked confused. "Why so? He's a pretty decent tipper."

"He *likes* your food?" Shelby asked, astonished.

"Sure. He wolfs it down. That's why I get good tips, and why I remember him."

Shelby was very confused now. "But that's really odd," she said softly, her mind going back to the conversation with the waiter at Chez Luis. What had he said?

"No," the waiter admitted. "But I remember him very well. He ordered the special last night—red snapper in a delicate pepper sauce. He complained that it was too salty, and demanded that I take it back and have the chef redo it. He was . . ." The man looked faintly embarrassed. "Let's say he was less than polite *about the whole matter. He's not someone I'd be likely to forget.''*

That didn't sound like the same man Will was talking about. Shelby had thought Pitt was a gourmet, and yet he ate *here*. . . . She told them all about the conversation, and Will shook his head in amazement.

''That guy makes like a snowstorm with the salt. He even adds more to the fries.''

''That doesn't make any sense,'' Cindi complained. ''If he eats the food here and adds salt, why on earth would he complain about the food at a swank place like that?''

Shelby was starting to get an idea. It didn't *sound* very logical that he'd complain about really well-prepared food, unless . . . ''Unless he *wanted* to be certain that the waiter remembered him,'' she said excitedly. ''It's a busy restaurant, and the waiter probably wouldn't normally remember him. *Unless* he made a real pain of himself, so that the waiter couldn't forget.''

''But why would he do that?'' Noah objected.

''The only reason I can think of,'' Shelby said, ''is that he *knew* he would need an alibi. Which meant he'd have had to know that the robbery was going to take place, and when it would take place."

"So you mean *he* stole the rock?" asked Cindi, excitedly.

"No," Shelby replied. "Quite the opposite. If he was establishing an alibi for himself, it means he *can't* have stolen the rock."

"Then it doesn't help us at all," Noah complained.

"Yes it does," Shelby answered. "If I'm right, and he complained to the waiter to make an alibi, then it means that Pitt knows who the real thief is, and is working with him or her."

"All right," Cindi said, grinning. "So we now know that Pitt is the thief's accomplice."

"*If* I'm right," Shelby corrected her. "I mean, it does make sense, but I could be missing something here. Still, if Pitt was in on the theft, *why* did he help steal the rock? And who's his partner in crime?" Her voice trailed off as she realized something. "Wait a minute. *Pitt* knows the alarm combination."

"So?" asked Cindi.

"Well, his partner doesn't have to be someone who works at the museum, then. It could be an outsider, and Pitt simply gave whoever it was the combination for the alarm."

Cindi pulled a face. "You've just opened up the whole thing," she complained. "Pitt's partner in crime could be anyone in Cocoa Beach! How do we narrow it down?"

"I think the most obvious way would be to follow Pitt and see if he meets up with anyone." Shelby grinned at her friends. "I think it's time for some undercover work tonight. Noah, do you think you'll be able to trail Pitt when he leaves the museum?"

"I'll need a disguise." He was happy now, planning his latest role.

Shelby felt elated. At last, they were on to something! She had a suspect! And now she had a call to make. . . .

Chapter
7

The house stood back from the road, behind a picket fence clearly meant to be ornamental rather than functional. The lawns were precisely the right height and shade of green. Shrubs and plants looked well tended and exactly where they ought to be for maximum effect. The gravel driveway looked as if it had been neatly swept—which, for all Shelby knew, it might. It was a house such as you might see in a magazine feature or on a TV show on lifestyles. It contrasted incredibly with the rougher but friendlier Rivers home. And Shelby knew that indoors would be the same as outside—everything precisely where it should be, neat, tidy, and virtually lifeless. She felt very out of place here, as if she were contaminating the grounds just by being a teenager.

She rang the doorbell, half expecting an English butler to open it and sneer down his nose at her. Instead, it was opened by a very attractive woman in what had to be a very expensive pants suit. "Yes?" the woman asked, raising a perfect eyebrow.

"Mrs. Cox?" Shelby asked. "Uh, I'm Shelby Woo. I go to school with your daughter, Brittany. Could I just see her for a moment?" Shelby knew she was blushing, as if she'd committed some crime herself.

Mrs. Cox eyed her indifferently, and then opened the door slightly wider, allowing Shelby to slink inside. She stood just inside the door, afraid that if she went farther she'd be accused of tracking dirt across the polished wooden floor. "Wait here," Mrs. Cox ordered, and walked away.

As Shelby had suspected, the house looked just as sterile inside as out. There were pedestals with statues, and the inevitable glass chandelier. A large staircase led to the upper floor, and two passages on either side of it led to other rooms. None of the adjoining doors stood open, and there wasn't the whisper of music or people anywhere. This was a house to look at, not to live in. Shelby hated it.

A moment later, Brittany came out of one of the rooms down the hall. She looked puzzled as she hurried over to join Shelby, which was understandable. After all, the two of them were hardly friends.

"Hi," Shelby said in a low voice. "Can we talk, Brittany? It's very important."

"Uh, sure." The blond girl still looked bemused, but she led the way to the closest door. "In the study."

The study looked as if it had been lifted from the Library of Congress. The walls were lined with bookcases, all filled and neatly dusted. There were two large desks, both holding only desk organizers and large blotters.

"Look, Brittany," she said quickly. "This is very important. It's about Tom."

Brittany flushed slightly, glancing back at the door that she had closed behind her. "Tom?" she said, obviously trying to act surprised. "Which Tom would that be?"

"You *know* which Tom," Shelby replied. "Don't play games. I saw your letters to him, and talked to him."

"Why?" demanded Brittany, coloring again. "It's none of your business. *Please* don't tell my parents!"

"Brittany, calm down," Shelby ordered. "Get a grip!" When the other girl nodded and took a deep breath, Shelby patted her hand. "I'm not going to tell your parents anything," she promised. "That's between you and them, but I don't think it's right to keep it from them. Still, that's your decision, not mine. I came to tell you that Tom's in danger of being arrested and charged with theft."

Brittany went white this time. "What?" she asked in a strangled voice.

Shelby quickly explained about the robbery. "So, you see, Tom won't tell the police where he was last night because it might get you into trouble with your parents. I promised him I wouldn't tell the police what he told me, but I didn't say I wouldn't tell you. So . . . it's up to you. Are you going to let him be all noble and get into trouble and maybe jail? Or will you tell the police he was with you?"

Brittany looked anguished. "Then my parents will find out," she said. "You don't know what they're like, Shelby."

Shelby looked around the room. "I think I have some idea," she answered, sympathetically. "They plan everything, and throw fits if things don't go exactly the way they want."

"Almost." Brittany nearly managed a smile. "They stand you in front of them like you're three years old and tell you how bitterly you've disappointed them, and how everything they've done is purely for your own good and that when you're older and wiser you'll certainly see that." She shook her head. "They make me feel like a pet dog that's chewed their slippers."

"It must be rough," Shelby said. "But can you just abandon Tom because of them?"

Brittany shook her head firmly. "No. I know I'm going to get into trouble because of it, but I'm going to tell the police the truth. I can't let Tom stay in jail when he didn't do anything. Come on, we'd better go before I lose my nerve."

Shelby followed Brittany down the hallway to a smaller, airier room, where Mrs. Cox sat reading a journal and making notes. She glanced up when the two girls entered the room.

"I have to go out for a short while, Mother," Brittany said meekly. "But when I return, I think I may need to speak with you."

Mrs. Cox examined a small, expensive watch. "I have to leave in two hours," she replied. "If you're later than that, we'll have to talk in the morning."

There was no good-bye or any kind of affection from her as they left. Shelby didn't want to criticize Brittany's parents, but she wasn't impressed. Brittany seemed to understand this, and simply shrugged.

Brittany seemed to be so relieved that someone finally knew about her and Tom. She told me about their dates, and about how much she liked Tom because he was so passionately committed to his goals, and so caring about his mother. He was completely different from the emotionless world Brittany had grown up in, and she felt when she was with him that she'd finally come to life.

"It sounds to me like he's really good for you," Shelby commented.

"He is," Brittany replied. "And good to me.

But I know my parents would hate him. He's so . . ."

"Black?" suggested Shelby.

"Actually, no, that's not the problem," Brittany said with a frown. "It's that he's *working class*. Poor. What they would consider to be a bad match. They see me marrying a surgeon, or a senator, or someone *important*. Their idea of important, of course, and not mine. For their only daughter to be dating someone who wants to become an astronaut would be totally ludicrous to them."

"So what are you going to do about it?" asked Shelby, feeling sorry for her.

"I'm going to have to tell them the truth," Brittany said simply. "And I know they're not going to like it."

Shelby suspected that Brittany was absolutely correct. They walked the rest of the way in silence. Inside the station, Shelby took Brittany over to Sergeant Ramirez and introduced her. "Brittany has something to tell you," she said, and glanced encouragingly at the other girl.

"Uh, Tom Rivers was out with me last night," she said, flushing.

Ramirez looked surprised, and then patted

Shelby's arm. "Thanks. Look, will you wait here? I'll take an official statement, and then I'm pretty sure we can get Tom to talk. I don't know what this is all about, but I hope you can explain." Ramirez led Brittany off to one of the interview rooms, leaving Shelby at her desk alone.

Which was kind of dull. Shelby fidgeted in the chair for a moment or two, wondering how long it would be, and then couldn't resist peeking at what the sergeant had been working on. It was the report from the fingerprints team at the museum. Shelby looked around quickly, but nobody in the office was paying her any attention. They were all used to seeing her there, after all. Then she picked up the report and skimmed it quickly.

It took her a few minutes to read through, but it pretty much boiled down to the fact that they'd found nothing of interest at the scene. There were no fingerprints on the glass fragments at all. For a moment, this puzzled Shelby. After all, there should have been some from Dave Pitt or Morgan Kane, and whoever had set up the case. Then she realized that these would have been cleaned off for the opening the next day.

This made Sergeant Ramirez's theory of its being an inside job a little stronger. How else could the alarm have been bypassed? And then I remembered . . .

"Somebody turned off the building's alarm. They knew the password, it seems. It looks like an inside job."

That had been Detective Hineline, talking about the burglary at Kemp's! That had looked like an inside job, too. Someone had turned off the burglar alarm at the store and then stolen the jewels. Someone had turned off the alarm at the museum and stolen the rock. . . .

Could it have been the *same* person?

Then Sergeant Ramirez came out of the interview room, with Brittany and Tom in tow. "Shelby!" she called. "Your friends can go now. They both tell the same story, now that Tom has talked, and I think we can let him go."

Shelby was happy. She walked out with the two of them. "Now what?" she asked Brittany.

"Now I have to tell my parents before they hear about this from someone else," Brittany said reluctantly. Her hand clasped Tom's. "Tom's coming with me for moral support. And maybe if they meet him, they may even like him. Though that's a big *maybe*."

"Good luck," Shelby offered, and watched them leave. She checked her watch and was astonished to discover it was almost six in the evening. The day had been so packed, it had gone very quickly. She was due back home now, so she hurried back to the Easterly Breeze.

Grandpa Mike looked up from his dusting with mild reproof. "You were supposed to help me with the housework," he reminded her gently.

"I know, and I'm going to get busy right now," Shelby promised. She felt very bad about having let her grandfather down. "But . . ."

"But you've become interested in another case," her grandfather finished for her. "I know you so well, Shelby. You have my own curiosity and energy. So, tell me about it while you help with the dusting."

Shelby did so, and Grandpa Mike listened carefully, nodding now and then. When she had finished, he cocked his head to one side.

"And do you have any ideas who might be

guilty, and, perhaps more important, *why* they took the rock?"

"Only a little," Shelby admitted. "I think that it must be one of the people who works at the museum. From his behavior at the restaurant, I'd say Dave Pitt *must* be involved, but obviously not alone. But is he working with Morgan or Dr. Burgess, or with someone else unconnected to the museum? And what about the jewelry theft at Kemp's? Can it be just a coincidence that it was robbed the same night? And that this Phantom, or whoever, turned off the alarm there? There's *got* to be a connection."

Grandpa Mike shook his head. "No, Shelby, you're going at this the wrong way. You've come up with a theory and you're trying to make the facts match it. You have to do it the other way around, or you'll make a mistake."

"But it *can't* be a coincidence," Shelby insisted.

"On the contrary," her grandfather replied. "It is possible that it is a coincidence. Not very likely, perhaps, but a good investigator should never make any assumptions. Make room for the possibility that the two crimes are unconnected." Then he smiled. "But don't overlook the fact that they may be joined."

Shelby, chastised, nodded. "You're right," she agreed. "But I still don't have any real idea *why* the rock was taken. I mean, I can see why a crook would rob a jewelry store. That stuff's valuable and can be sold almost anywhere. But why steal a Martian rock that nobody is likely to buy?"

"There are reasons for stealing other than immediate gain," her grandfather answered.

"Yes, I remember your lessons," Shelby assured him. "There's also revenge or insanity. But I don't see how they fit, either."

"Ah." Grandpa Mike gave a small smile. "Good, but that's not what I meant. You're assuming that the point of stealing the rock was to *possess* the rock. But is that necessarily true? Does the absence of the rock do anything?" He gestured at the TV, which was turned off now. "There was an item on the local news about the theft, and I noticed that there were a number of people who seemed to have gone to the museum to see the scene of the crime."

Shelby realized what he was getting at. "A publicity stunt?" she asked. Was that possible? She thought about Kane and his love of making a profit. Well, she wouldn't put anything past him. He was greedy enough to rob even his own museum for some free publicity.

Then she shook her head. "Then why break the case containing the rock?" she asked. "If he stole the rock himself, he could just have taken it out and left the case intact. . . ."

I remembered what Kane had said earlier:

"On our last stop in Chicago, Dave accidentally broke the case by hitting it with a crowbar when we were dismantling some exhibits. I had to have it replaced then. The stupid thing seems to be always causing me trouble."

"In fact, he seemed almost more annoyed about the case being broken than about the rock being stolen," Shelby explained. "So I don't think he'd have broken the case. On the other hand . . . Dr. Burgess had mentioned that the rock was insured."

Grandpa Mike smiled happily. "Now you have something to think about while you're dusting," he told her. "But don't forget to dust while you think!"

Shelby nodded, setting to work. It certainly

helped to make the work go faster. Grandpa Mike had made a small suggestion, but one worth thinking about. Maybe the rock hadn't been stolen for its own value. Maybe there was another sort of value in stealing it—like insurance money, or publicity, or even something she hadn't thought of yet.

She had a lot to consider.

Chapter
8

Noah stared raptly at the door to the space museum. He was hiding in the shadows of an adjacent store's alley. He'd disguised himself in a curly blond wig and a drooping mustache, trying to look like one of the slightly older crowd who hung around the beach all summer until school opened again. This way, if Pitt did spot him, he wouldn't recognize him.

Dr. Burgess had left ten minutes earlier, carrying her laptop computer. She strode briskly away toward her hotel. Noah waited, and then grinned as Pitt and Kane both left the building, locking the door carefully behind them. Now . . .

were they going to the Easterly Breeze together, or were they splitting up?

Kane said something, and started down the road. Pitt stood still for a moment, then turned and started walking toward the alley. Noah gave a start and hugged the shadows of the wall more closely. To his relief, Pitt walked past the alley without a glance. Noah gave him a moment, then peered out after him. He was walking quickly down the street. Noah slid out of the shadows and started to follow him.

It was nine o'clock, but in the summer that didn't mean too much in Cocoa Beach. There were plenty of people around, so Noah was pretty sure he was inconspicuous. Pitt never looked back, and he was walking with somewhere in mind.

It was C.J.'s, in fact. Pitt entered, obviously aiming to get something to eat. Noah wished he could go in, too, but he didn't dare. Not that he expected a problem with Pitt, but everyone who worked at C.J.'s knew Noah. Even though his disguise was good, he couldn't risk one of them recognizing him and making a fuss about it that could alert Pitt. So he forced himself to wait outside, trying to ignore the burger and cola that were calling his name. He did creep up to the window to check that Pitt was eating alone, and not meeting someone, though. Pitt had a small table to himself, and a large burger and fries. He added extra salt, too.

Thankfully, Pitt wasn't too long. He obviously did like the food there. As he started off again, Noah fell into step behind him, trying not to get too close. Pitt headed down the street, stopping now and then to look in shop windows. It looked like he was heading back to the Easterly Breeze, but Noah had to be certain about that.

Then Pitt took a quick left, taking him away from the right road. Noah felt excitement mounting. Maybe he *was* meeting his partner in crime, after all! He hurried around the corner after his target, and stopped.

There was nobody in the small side street at all.

Noah couldn't understand it. He'd seen Pitt turn down here. . . . He *couldn't* have lost him! Maybe he'd entered one of the buildings in this street? But which one? Noah moved forward to check.

And there was an arm about his neck, tight

against his throat. Noah gave a strangled bleat as the pressure increased.

"What's the idea?" a voice hissed in his ear. "Are you trying to rob me?"

Noah couldn't answer, because he couldn't breathe. He tried to break free of the headlock, but it was impossible. The man who held him was simply much too strong for him. Noah struggled, but the grip was implacable. He couldn't breathe, and his lungs felt like they were on fire. There were red blotches in front of his eyes. He clawed at the arm around his throat, trying to break free, but the man who held him shook him.

And his wig came loose.

"What the devil?" the man grunted in surprise. Then his arm let up a little, and Noah was able to take in a gigantic breath. The man tore his wig off, and then whipped Noah around to stare at his face. "What's going on?" His free hand came up and ripped loose the fake mustache. "What's the big idea?"

Noah caught his breath, and tried to clear his foggy head. "I'm just practicing," he said, gasping. "I'm an actor. Playing a detective. I just wanted to see if I could follow someone without being seen."

The man was Pitt, of course. "Then you're terrible at it," he growled. His eyes narrowed. "I get a feeling I've seen you before somewhere."

"Maybe you've caught one of my plays?" Noah suggested. "I was in *Man and Superman* last month."

"Well, I hope you weren't playing Superman," Pitt snapped. "You'd have done research for that by trying to leap tall buildings in a single bound."

"Hey, that's good," Noah replied. He was back to normal now. "Uh, can I have my mustache back?"

Pitt grunted, but gave it over. "Kid, you're screwy. And I don't like being bothered. So, get lost. Now. Or else I'll see to it that the only part you'll get from now on is as the Hunchback of Notre Dame." He raised a large fist. "Understand?"

"Definitely," Noah said, backing off. " 'Bye." He turned and hurried away. Well, he'd really blown this one. He couldn't trail Pitt anymore. He'd have to admit to Shelby that he was a failure.

On the bright side, though, at least he could get himself that burger now.

The following morning, Shelby arranged to meet up with Cindi and Noah, and then went off to the space museum. She still had her pass, and maybe taking another look at the place would give her some ideas.

It was hardly busy. There were about six people inside, wandering around and looking at the exhibits. Kane was there, surveying his customers glumly. He scowled at Shelby as she went over to greet him. "I guess business isn't so hot," she remarked, trying to be sympathetic.

Kane grunted. "You'd think there'd be more interest in space in a town so close to the Cape," he grumbled. "And after the publicity we got from the robbery." He gestured at the few people there. "If it keeps up like this, I won't be able to afford to stay open. I'm losing money." He glared at her. "Haven't the police even managed to find my rock yet?"

"Not as far as I know," Shelby replied. "But I know they're doing their best."

"Well, it's not very good," complained Kane. "I mean, they've had the thief under arrest for *hours*. He should have told them something by now."

"If you're referring to Tom Rivers," Shelby informed him cheerfully, "you're wrong on both counts. He's not a thief and he's not under arrest."

"What?" Kane looked like a volcano ready to explode. "What are you talking about? I *know* the police arrested him."

"They took him in for *questioning*," Shelby answered. "His girlfriend, Brittany Cox, told the police he was out with her last night, so they knew he was innocent."

Kane growled, and shook his head. "She's lying just to cover up for him!" he yelled. "Any moron can see that! I'm going down to the station right now and I'm going to give that dumb cop a piece of my mind." He stomped off across the room and out the door.

"I just hope you can spare a piece," Shelby muttered. He really had it in for poor Tom! Well, she doubted that he'd manage to intimidate Sergeant Ramirez. Putting him out of her mind for now, she headed for the broken exhibit case. She found Dave Pitt there, and the case almost fixed. Noah had told her about his run-in with Pitt last night, and that he didn't seem to have remembered who Noah was, thankfully. Otherwise he might not have been so friendly to Shelby.

"There we go," he said happily, placing the glass back on the case. "And all we need now is the rock to put in it." He gave Shelby a friendly smile. "You think that's likely to happen soon?"

"It's hard to say," Shelby replied, admiring his work. "That's as good as new."

"Better," Pitt said proudly. He gave the base a thump, and it didn't even move. "It's a lot more solid than it was, now that I've repaired it. It should stand up to almost any knocks now." He sighed, and glanced around the almost deserted exhibition hall. "Just in time to pack it up and move on again, it looks like. Business isn't too good here."

"Yes," Shelby agreed. "Mr. Kane said he was losing money."

Pitt shrugged. "He always says that, but somehow he always comes up with some from somewhere to keep going. He's very dedicated to this museum. Well, I've got other things to do. See you around—maybe." He nodded pleasantly and moved off.

Kane was always complaining that he was losing money? Then how could he afford to stay in business? Renting this property, paying for the utilities, and having both Pitt and Dr. Burgess to pay couldn't be cheap. Yet there weren't many paying customers. Unless he had some other way of making money off the museum?

Ideas were starting to sparkle inside Shelby's head, but she needed more information. Had he put in a claim for the stolen Martian rock? There was somebody who could probably tell him the answer to that—Dr. Burgess. She'd mentioned that it was her job to file the insurance claim. Shelby headed for the back rooms, and tapped on the scientist's door before entering.

Dr. Burgess was there, working on her computer. She glanced up and seemed a little annoyed to see Shelby. This vanished, to be replaced by a smile. "Shelly, isn't it?" she asked, pleasantly enough.

"Shelby," she corrected. She glanced at the computer screen, and then blinked. It was showing a page from the Downey Insurance Company records, and was flashing a request for a password.

Dr. Burgess saw what Shelby was looking at, and gave a nervous laugh. "That's our insurance company," she explained. "I was just trying to see if they'd put through the claim for the stolen rock yet. But, as you can see, I need a password to get in. And, naturally, I don't have one." She started to shut down the operation.

So they *had* filed a claim! "I don't think they allow customers to check like that," Shelby said, frowning.

"Well, I guess not," agreed Dr. Burgess, getting back to her main menu. "It was rather silly of me to look, wasn't it?"

"I imagine."

Dr. Burgess gave her a shrewd look. "Is there something I can do for you, Shelby?" she asked.

"Thanks, but I think I have the answer I was looking for," Shelby replied. "Well, I guess you're kind of busy. I'd better leave you to it."

Now what? Shelby checked her watch, and discovered it was time to meet with Cindi and Noah. She hurried over to the meeting, wondering if she'd managed to get further with a solution, or only deeper into questions. Sharing a pizza with her friends, she brought them up to date.

"So do you believe this story Dr. Burgess told you?" asked Cindi.

"You'd have to have rocks for brains to believe *that*," sneered Noah. "The woman was trying to hack into the insurance company's records, if you ask me. If Shelby had arrived a few moments later, she'd have caught her at it."

"Maybe," agreed Shelby. "But we don't *know* that was what she was trying to do. She may just have been naive enough to think she could get the files she wanted. Sometimes the brightest people do the dumbest things."

"Especially if her mind's on space, not on the real world," added Cindi. "It sounds to me like she was just trying to be superefficient and impress her boss. Don't forget, he's losing money, and that's just one step away from laying people off."

"That's true," Shelby said, realizing it was something she should have thought of herself. "And she'd been laid off from her last job, which she obviously took badly. To be laid off again might be more than she could stomach. So I suppose it *is* possible she was just trying to impress

Kane with her abilities so he wouldn't even think of firing her." She sighed. "Which doesn't get us any closer to a solution to this mystery. Except it makes me even more certain than ever that Tom didn't do it."

"Speaking of whom," Noah announced, "I called him this morning to see how things went last night with Brittany's parents." He shook his head. "I gather they all but bodily threw Tom out, and they've grounded Brittany for her next several lives. Talk about strict parents!"

"The poor guy," Shelby said sadly. "And Brittany, too. I saw what her life's like. It's worse than prison in some ways."

"I guess rich people don't always have the most fun, then," Cindi observed. "Mind you, I'd like the chance to be rich just to see."

It seemed to Shelby to be very unfair, but there wasn't anything she could do about it. Brittany's parents had the right to tell their daughter what to do until she left home. But Shelby was absolutely certain that they were wrong. Grandpa Mike would never forbid her to go on dates. Except she didn't really date. She was too busy right now. Speaking of which . . . "I guess I'd better be going," she said, finishing the last of her slice of pizza and washing it down with cola.

"What's next on the case?" asked Cindi.

"The more I think about it, the more it seems to me that there's a link between the theft of the Martian rock and the jewelry robbery. Maybe this Phantom person is behind both. If I can just get some idea of who the Phantom might be, maybe it'll help me figure out who our thief is."

"Good luck, then," Cindi replied. "Well, if you need our help, you know how to reach us. Come on, Noah, we'd better get back to the store. Lots more beach pictures to develop and print."

Shelby headed off to the police station. It wasn't a day she was supposed to work, but she hoped she'd get a chance to look at the information about the Phantom. She knew that Detective Hineline wouldn't show her, but maybe Sergeant Ramirez might if she was asked right . . . if she had to ask. With luck, she could just take a peek at the file without needing to ask permission.

Luck was with her. When she arrived at the station, it was almost deserted. She quickly checked the files on Detective Hineline's desk. Since he always left them for her to file away, the one on the Phantom was there, as she'd suspected it would be. Guiltily, she ducked over to her own desk and started to skim through the information.

The first thing she saw was a copy of the business card. As the detective had said, it was one of those you simply ran off a laser printer. Anyone could make one, so it wasn't much of a clue. After that, there was a list of all the places the Phantom had struck. They were scattered all over the country. The last one had been two weeks earlier in Chicago. There didn't seem to be any pattern in the crimes at all, except they were always jewelry stores, and in every case the burglar alarms had been turned off. The police would never have known they were all done by the same person if it wasn't for the calling card.

Which meant that the Phantom *wanted* them to know it was him every time.

There was a short report sketching out theories from the FBI as to who the Phantom might be. Shelby gave it a quick read, but there wasn't much. Someone who was very technologically smart. Someone who enjoyed taunting the police with how clever he was and the police weren't.

Someone quite fit. It could be describing lots of people.

There was the sound of someone clearing their throat, and Shelby looked up guiltily, expecting to see Detective Hineline. Luckily, it was Sergeant Ramirez instead, but she was frowning.

"Shelby, what are you doing?" she asked. She held out her hand. "You're supposed to file them, not read them."

"I know," Shelby admitted, handing back the folder. "But I just wanted to check out the Phantom, and see what the police know."

"Not enough," Ramirez replied wryly. "And it doesn't look like we're getting very far on this latest case, either. But I don't think Detective Hineline wants your help in solving his case, Shelby."

"No, I wasn't thinking of that," Shelby admitted. "I was thinking of it for *my* case." She blushed as she realized what she'd just said. "Well, your case, really. The theft of the Mars rock. You see, in *both* cases, the alarm systems were turned off."

"That's the only similarity," the sergeant answered with a laugh. "I don't think the same person who steals half a million dollars' worth of jewels is going to steal an old piece of rock that's virtually unsellable."

"Maybe not," agreed Shelby. "But I just thought that there *might* be a connection."

"Take it from me, Shelby, there isn't." Ramirez smiled. "In fact, you needn't even bother worrying about the theft of the rock any longer. We've got it back, and the thief with it."

"You have?" Shelby's eyes went wide. She felt pleased and disappointed at the same time. Pleased that the crook had been caught, but bitterly disappointed that she hadn't done it—in fact, that she still really didn't have much of an idea as to who it was. "So *who* is it?"

"Tom Rivers," said Ramirez smugly.

Hardly able to believe her ears, Shelby gasped: "Tom Rivers! But . . . he *can't* be the thief. He just can't."

Ramirez raised an eyebrow. "I'm sorry to disappoint you, Shelby," she said, "but there's no doubt at all. Tom has just finished giving us a full confession."

Chapter
9

Shelby was glad that she was sitting down, because she'd gone weak all over. Tom guilty? How could she have been so wrong? She had been absolutely certain he was innocent, and yet . . .

"Don't take it so badly, Shelby," Ramirez said gently, placing a hand on Shelby's shoulder. "Sometimes people we trust do let us down."

Shelby considered this, but she still couldn't buy it. Tom seemed so honest, and so concerned. "How did it all happen?" she asked, trying to understand it.

"It started with an anonymous call," the sergeant replied, sitting down close to Shelby. "Someone called to say that they'd just read about the theft in the morning papers, and they remembered seeing a black teenager hiding a rock." She shrugged. "I don't normally like anonymous tips, but I couldn't ignore it. So I went to where the tipster said the rock had been hidden, and found it in about five minutes." She gave Shelby a sympathetic look. "It was in a gazebo on a piece of property belonging to a couple of lawyers named Cox."

Shelby stared at her. "Brittany's house?" she said, completely confused.

"Right. I remembered the address from when Brittany gave us her statement yesterday. Finding the rock gave me enough to bring in Brittany and Tom for questioning." She sighed. "Tom realized that they had been caught, and he confessed to the whole thing. He said he'd stolen the rock to get even with Kane for firing him, and that he'd hidden it at the Coxes' house without their knowledge. And that he'd convinced Brittany to lie to cover up for him."

Shelby thought this through for a moment or two and then shook her head. "I don't believe it."

Ramirez patted her shoulder again. "I know it's hard to accept, but—"

"No," Shelby insisted. "I don't believe it. It doesn't fit the facts. I've talked to both Tom and Brittany, and this just isn't like them. Brittany isn't very good at telling lies. She's too honest. And Tom's just as bad. I think he's just telling you what you want to hear." A thought occurred to her and she snapped her fingers. "I'll bet he gave you his confession *after* you promised that Brittany wouldn't be charged with anything, right?"

The sergeant's eyes narrowed. "So?"

"So he's trying to keep her out of trouble again," Shelby explained. "That was why he wouldn't talk earlier, remember? If they'd agreed she'd lie to cover up for him, why didn't he give us his alibi straightaway? Because he was trying to protect her, that's why. And I think he's trying to do it again. He's confessing to the theft to stop you from charging Brittany with it."

Ramirez considered the idea for a moment. "Maybe," she finally agreed. "It does make some sort of sense."

"And I think I can prove he's innocent," Shelby added. She knew she was taking a bit of a risk now, but she still believed Tom's story—his original one, that is. "Let me ask him just one question, and I bet I can prove he's innocent."

Ramirez chuckled. "You don't give up, do you, Shelby? Okay, I'll see if I can convince Detective Hineline to allow you to ask one question. Come on." She led the way to the interview room, tapped on the door, and entered. Shelby followed her inside.

Tom was there, looking very tired and worried. Hineline was sitting close by him, a grim expression on his face. There was also a police secretary there, with a video camera, who'd obviously been recording the confession.

"What is it?" Hineline asked. He glanced at Shelby. "I might have known you'd be here."

"Shelby thinks she can help us with this case," Ramirez replied.

"What a surprise," grumbled Hineline, rolling his eyes. "Shelby *always* thinks she can help us."

"I know," Shelby said, meekly. "But there's just one question I'd like Tom to answer, if he's really guilty of this theft."

Tom glared at her defiantly. "I *am* guilty. Now leave me alone. I've already told the police everything."

Hineline glowered at her, but curiosity finally got the better of him. "What question?" he finally asked.

Shelby grinned happily, and turned to Tom. "You stole the Martian rock on Friday night, right?"

"That's the question?" Hineline grumbled.

"Yes, I did," Tom said, sitting up straight. "And you can't prove otherwise."

"Yes I can," Shelby answered. "If you stole the rock—then what's the combination to turn off the alarm system?"

I was gambling a little bit here. Pitt had said he thought that Tom had stolen the combination while he was in Kane's office on Friday. But Tom had claimed he was looking for proof that some of the exhibits were fakes. I was willing to bet that if he'd seen the combination, he wouldn't have been at all interested in memorizing it.

Tom looked confused for a second, and then angry. "I don't have to answer that," he said.

"No," agreed Hineline, sitting forward

slightly. "But if you don't, I'd like to know *why* you won't."

"I've said all I'm going to," Tom insisted. He glared at Shelby. "And I'm not talking in front of her. She's got no right to be here."

"You're right." Hineline didn't even look around. "Shelby—out."

Shelby was annoyed by his abrupt dismissal, but she knew better than to argue. Meekly, she left the interview room, but she felt very elated. Tom had refused to answer her question—*because he couldn't*. He didn't know the combination. Because he hadn't really stolen anything at all.

So, someone else was the thief. Someone who disliked Tom enough to frame him for the job. But who? And why?

And then I realized that the *real* thief had made a very bad mistake. If I was right, and Tom was innocent, then someone must have framed him. And I was sure that only one person could have done that. But could I prove it?

Her friends met up with her at C.J.'s as usual. "Tom's been arrested," she informed them.

"He's confessed to the crime to try and keep Brittany out of trouble again."

"Boy, he's a glutton for punishment," Noah commented.

Cindi smacked his arm. "He's in love," she said. "He's trying to protect his girl from trouble. I think it's rather romantic, really."

"I think it's rather dumb," Noah responded. "He should just tell the truth."

"I think you're both a bit right," Shelby informed them. "But I know who framed Tom, and that means I know who stole the Martian rock in the first place."

"Who?" asked Noah and Cindi in chorus.

"Morgan Kane," Shelby replied.

"Kane?" Noah was confused. "How come?"

Because after the police let Tom go yesterday, I went to the museum. I talked to Kane, to Pitt, and to Dr. Burgess. But the only one I told the news about Tom to was Morgan Kane. And when I told him about it, he got very angry and went off in a rage. So he was the only suspect who knew that Tom wasn't in jail.

Cindi nodded thoughtfully after Shelby explained this. "And you think he *actually* went off to plant the rock and get Tom into trouble."

"Right." Shelby looked a little sheepish. "I was the one who told him that Tom was dating Brittany Cox. He must have realized that he could get Tom into worse trouble by planting the evidence at Brittany's, rather than at Tom's. He didn't know if the police had already searched Tom's house or not, because I didn't tell him. But he must have known they hadn't looked at Brittany's."

Noah nodded. "That makes sense so far," he agreed. "But why would Kane steal his own rock in the first place and want to frame Tom?"

"Two reasons," Shelby explained. "First of all, his museum is losing money. He needed some publicity to make people want to come to it. A robbery of the Martian rock was pretty good for headlines. Only it wasn't the top headline. There was the big jewelry case, which overshadowed his own robbery. So he didn't get as much publicity as he wanted. And the other reason was that he has the rock insured. If it never turned up again, he'd get a lot of money to pay for it."

Cindi broke in. "Okay so far," she said. "But

then why did he plant the rock where it would be found? Surely that means he can't claim on the insurance?"

"That's right," agreed Shelby. "But there's the other aspect of his game to consider. Tom Rivers claimed that Kane has deliberately been faking some of his exhibits, and that he was going to prove it. I think Tom was right, and Kane knew it. If it turned out that some of his stuff is faked, there'd be a big scandal, and his museum would probably be closed down. He lives for the show, and he couldn't stand the thought. So he had to make Tom's accusations sound as if they were wrong. Framing him for the theft accomplishes that. I think discrediting Tom is more important to Kane right now than the insurance money."

Cindi nodded slowly. "Okay. I can see all of that. But how are we going to prove that Kane's behind the whole thing?"

"We go to the museum," Shelby replied. "I want to have another look at the case that used to hold the Martian rock. You see, there's still one thing I don't quite understand, and that's why the case was broken. Kane was very upset about that, and I don't think he was faking it.

112

But if he stole the rock, why would he break his own case?"

Noah agreed with her. "But it makes perfect sense if he and Pitt stole the rock," he said eagerly. "All they had to do was to take it when they closed the museum, and then claim it was still there when they locked up. Simple."

"True," agreed Shelby. "But why would he then smash the case? That's the part that doesn't make any sense. . . . Unless what I'm thinking is true. I think there was a very good reason to smash the case, and that it has nothing to do with the theft of the Mars rock. But we need proof of that." She grinned at Cindi. "Glad you've brought your camera, Cindi," she said. "You may have a few more pictures to take." Slinging her bag over her shoulder, she led the way to the museum. Using the passes Kane had given them, they entered.

As on the previous day, it was almost deserted. There was only one family looking around, and they left a few moments later. Shelby and her friends were the only ones in the museum now.

"Okay," Shelby said. "Let's take a look at the repaired case." They hurried over to it, and

Shelby examined it. Pitt had done a really good job with it, as he'd said. Since the Martian rock was now at the police station as evidence, the case was still empty.

"So what are we looking for?" asked Noah. "It's empty."

"Right," agreed Shelby. "But I don't think it's really empty at all. Just think for a minute. Why bother breaking the case if the alarm is turned off? There's no need to do it, is there? *Unless* you need a broken case for some reason." She gripped the glass top of the case. If the alarm was connected to the case, opening it would get her into real trouble. On the other hand, since the case was *supposed* to be empty, why would they need to connect an alarm up to it yet? And, besides, the alarms were turned off when the museum was open. She was *almost* certain of that. There was only one way to know for sure, though.

She lifted off the glass case, holding her breath.

Nothing. No alarm. She'd been right! Carefully, she set down the glass top, and then fiddled in her bag for her Swiss Army knife. She pulled out the screwdriver blade, and moved to unscrew the closest screw.

"Hey!" Kane yelled, hurrying into the room. "What the blazes do you kids think you're doing? Vandals! I'm calling the police on you!"

Shelby winced; how could she have been so dumb? It was a *silent* alarm, of course, which registered in the office, not out here. Noah and Cindi gulped, but looked to Shelby for guidance.

"Call the police," Shelby said coolly. "I'd love to see you explain what's in here to them."

"You?" growled Kane, as he came up to them. "What's with you? Why are you breaking my case again?"

"I'm not breaking it," Shelby replied. "I'm opening it." She showed him her knife. As she did so, she reached into her bag and found her tape recorder by touch. She started it recording, so she'd have proof for Detective Hineline.

"Why?" asked Kane. He looked genuinely puzzled, as well as angry. "It's empty."

Shelby was starting to have second thoughts. Had she made a mistake after all? But she couldn't have. She had to be right. All of her deductions made perfect sense. "It's not empty, and we both know it," she said. "Like we both know that it was *you* who framed Tom Rivers for stealing your Martian rock when it was you who took it in the first place. There wasn't any robbery. You were just trying to claim the insurance on it."

"What?" Kane tried to look innocent, but this time he was obviously faking it.

Emboldened by this, Shelby continued. "This museum's been losing money for a while, and you couldn't afford it anymore. So you decided to steal your own rock, and claim it on the insurance. You made it look like Tom Rivers had done it. Then you planted it at Brittany Cox's house to frame him even more."

Kane snorted. "That's an interesting theory," he said, "but if you're right, haven't I just lost the insurance money by doing that?"

"Yes," agreed Shelby. "But you've stopped anyone from believing that Tom was telling the truth about you faking some of these exhibits. You *know* that some of them are fakes, and you forced Dr. Burgess to say they weren't by threatening to fire her. She had no option but to cover up for you. And you had her checking on the insurance claim for you. She's terrified of being fired again, so you could get her to do whatever you wanted."

Kane shook his head. "You're incredible," he said, almost amused. "But that's a crazy theory. You haven't got any proof for any of it."

"I will have in a minute." Shelby turned to Cindi. "Be sure and take lots of photos, to prove we're not making this up."

"Making *what* up?" demanded Kane.

It had all come together when I realized that only Kane could have framed Tom. Kane could only have done that if he had the rock. Which meant that he had to have been behind the theft. So why, then, did he have to break the case? The answer had to be because he needed to make changes to it. Why? Well, there was the jewel robbery, and the fact that Kane always came up with money to keep his museum open.

"You're the Phantom," Shelby replied.

"The who?" he asked. "That comic-book character in purple tights? What are you talking about?"

"The jewel thief," Shelby said. "That's how

you've managed to keep the museum open. You rob jewelry stores to get the money."

Kane laughed, and this time it seemed genuine. "You really are flaky," he said. "I've never robbed anything in my life, and certainly not jewelry stores. Whatever makes you think I have?"

Shelby started to unscrew the base of the display stand. "The broken display case," she said.

"I'm prepared to take a lie detector test to prove that rock was here when I left on Friday night," Kane said. "I'd pass it, too." His eyes narrowed as Shelby took out the second screw.

Continuing her work, Shelby said: "The display case was broken to give you an excuse to fix it, and make it stronger. And heavier. So that nobody would be surprised that when it left it was heavier than when it came in. Because it would have extra weight inside." She finished taking out the screws, and then lifted off the top of the base.

Inside it lay exactly what she'd expected to see—a whole nest of gemstones, sparkling in the flash as Cindi took more pictures.

"Holy cow!" exclaimed Kane. "There really *are* stolen gems in there!"

Smugly, Shelby folded her arms and smiled at him. "Like I said, you're the Phantom."

"No he isn't," said a familiar voice. Shelby whirled around to see Dr. Burgess standing there, watching them. "I am. That idiot isn't capable of dreaming up a plan as clever as this one was."

Chapter
10

"You?" Shelby gasped. "But I thought he was just forcing you to do his dirty work."

Dr. Burgess rolled her eyes. "Please! He's an idiot. I used him as cover for my thefts. He didn't have a clue as to what was going on. Pitt and I just put up with him. This silly little scheme of his to steal his own Martian rock was as clever as he ever got. He never had a clue about the stolen gems."

Kane had gone white, and then red with anger. "You and Pitt were *using* me?" he howled. "You're fired!"

"You idiot," Dr. Burgess said, smiling nastily. "Do you really think I need your pathetic little job? With all the money I've made from my robberies, I could have retired a long time ago."

"So why didn't you?" asked Noah.

I felt like such an idiot! The facts had been there all along, but I hadn't added them together. The Phantom was supposed to be very arrogant, which Dr. Burgess was, and really smart. "He" was also good at breaking codes, just as I'd seen her attempting with the insurance company. I should have realized that she was the Phantom, and not Kane.

"Ego," Shelby said, realizing the truth. "She thinks she's better than everyone else, and she has to prove it. That's why she always left her calling cards as the Phantom. To gloat, and rub it in."

"I *am* superior," Dr. Burgess snapped. "I simply want other people to acknowledge the fact. Firing me was the stupidest thing NASA ever did. I've proven my genius over and over again since then. I've robbed dozens of stores, made a million dollars, and never been caught."

"Until now," Shelby pointed out.

Dr. Burgess shook her head. She reached for an exhibit beside her. It was some kind of space-welding equipment, which she held in her hand and then switched on. "This is a laser cutter. It can slice through steel in space, so it would have even nastier effects on your bodies. You're the ones who are not going to be talking."

Shelby's throat went dry as she realized that the woman was perfectly serious. She'd managed to get herself and her friends into very deep trouble here. Dr. Burgess wouldn't let them tell the police anything. "You can't possibly think about killing us," she said boldly. A trickle of sweat started to crawl down her spine.

"It may not come to that," agreed Dr. Burgess. "I have no real desire to hurt you. All I have to do is lock you up somewhere safe while I make my getaway." She smiled. "I know I can elude the police. I'm good at that sort of thing." She gestured with the cutter. "One at a time, I want you to come back here. There's a closet I can lock you all in. Someone will find you before you starve to death, I'm sure."

Kane stomped forward, obviously aiming to tear Dr. Burgess apart with his bare hands. She shook her head and held up the laser cutter. "Naughty, naughty," she chided. "Be smart."

Shelby started to follow Kane, her eyes flicking around for something she might be able to do. Anything . . .

The laser cutter, she realized, was electrical. And she could see the cord, just past Dr. Burgess. . . . As she moved to follow Kane, she pretended to stumble, and then fell to the floor. Quickly, she shot out her hand and then jerked at the cable.

The light on the cutter died.

Kane saw the shock in his ex-employee's eyes and jumped at her. With a cry, Dr. Burgess slammed the cutter down on his head, sending him reeling to the floor. But this gave Shelby time to get back to her feet, and she was ready to take over the fight.

"That's enough," said a familiar voice. "Time-out, everyone."

Shelby stared at the entrance to the museum.

Detective Hineline and Sergeant Ramirez were both there. She went almost weak with relief.

Dr. Burgess obviously considered her chances for a moment. Then she opened her hand and let the cutter drop. Finally, she seemed to slump in on herself.

"Thank you, Detective!" Shelby said gratefully.

Hineline stared at her. "You I'm going to talk to later," he promised. He didn't seem very unhappy with her, though.

Back at the police station, Shelby, Noah, and Cindi sat in the interview room telling their story to Detective Hineline and Sergeant Ramirez. Dr. Burgess, Pitt, and Kane were all in jail right now, and the jewels were in the evidence room.

"So I figured that Kane was the Phantom," Shelby explained. "And that was why he'd had the pedestal broken. But I was wrong, wasn't I?"

"Yes," Hineline replied. "But you were right in many ways. He *did* steal his own rock for the insurance, and he *did* frame Tom Rivers to stop him from talking. What happened on Friday night, though, was that he and Pitt locked the place up with the rock still there. They needed to be able to say they'd left it there in case we ran a lie detector test on them. After that, Burgess came back and stole the rock. She then broke the case—which she wasn't supposed to do, of course, and which irritated Kane so much—just as you figured, so Pitt would have to rebuild it and give them somewhere to hide the jewels."

"I figured that much out," Ramirez said. "You see, I had already guessed that Dr. Burgess was the Phantom. It couldn't have been Kane. Remember when he took you to see Dr. Burgess you told me that he almost wiped out one of her files because he's such a klutz on the computer. So he couldn't have used one to bypass the alarm systems at Kemp's. On the other hand, Dr. Burgess could. And the other clue for me was that Kane told us that the same case had been broken in Chicago, supposedly accidentally by Pitt. And Chicago was the last place where the Phantom had struck. Pitt broke the case so he could smuggle the jewels out the same way that he did here. He obviously liked the method, and just used it each time."

"Right," said Shelby, blushing. "I should have remembered those clues."

"You did pretty well," said Ramirez warmly. "I'd figured out that Dr. Burgess was the Phantom, and Detective Hineline simply matched up the travels of the space museum to the robberies, and they coincided exactly. We were on our way over to question Dr. Burgess when we stumbled onto your little scene."

"Your *stupid* little scene," Hineline growled. "You managed to get yourself and your friends into real trouble there. Who knows what that woman would have done if we hadn't arrested her?"

Shelby colored again. "I didn't expect anything like that to happen, Detective," she said. "I thought we could just open the case and get pictures of the gems. That way, you'd have the evidence you needed to arrest Kane and let Tom go."

"And that's *exactly* why I keep telling you to leave the mysteries to the police," complained Hineline. "Because you're not really prepared for what may happen. It's not always what you think, and sometimes it's very dangerous. I'm just worried about what might happen to you, Shelby."

Ramirez raised an eyebrow and looked at her boss. "On the other hand, she *did* prove that Kane was behind the rock theft and not the Rivers boy," she pointed out. "Which we hadn't figured out. So Shelby *was* right about that."

"Yes," agreed Cindi, backing up her friend. "She's a heroine."

"She's a pain in the behind," grumbled Hineline, but his heart didn't seem to be in it. "You're all lucky I don't charge you with interfering with police business. Anyway, I've ordered your friend released, so maybe you'd better go and see him." As they started to leave, he held out his hand. "Shelby, I want the tape you recorded of Dr. Burgess's confession. *And* that camera from your friend, so we have photographic proof of the whole thing."

"So you do need my help after all?" asked Shelby innocently, as she handed over her cassette.

"Out," growled Hineline.

Outside the room, Cindi managed a grin. "He's really not so bad, is he?" she asked.

"It's a good day for him," Shelby answered.

"He's caught the elusive Phantom, and that'll make him the envy of dozens of other policemen who couldn't manage it."

"Hey, guys!" yelled Tom across the room, hurrying over to them. "I heard that you got me cleared, and that Kane actually confessed he'd been the one who'd stolen the rock. Thanks, guys. I owe you big time for this."

"That's okay," said Shelby happily. "I'm glad we could help." She grinned. "I think this is the first case I've ever had where *all* of the suspects were guilty of something—except for the one that the police thought was guilty!"

They left the police station together. As they did, Tom stopped dead in his path. Shelby, Cindi, and Noah came to a halt with him.

Waiting for them were Brittany Cox and her mother.

"Tom!" Brittany said with relief. To his embarrassment and delight, she grabbed hold of him and hugged him hard. "I'm so glad you've been set free."

"Me too," agreed Tom, hardly taking a breath. "But I thought that you were grounded for life?"

Brittany turned and looked at her mother, without saying anything.

Somewhat embarrassed, Mrs. Cox cleared her throat. "Brittany told me what you did," she said. "That you confessed to a crime you didn't commit to keep her out of trouble. That was very foolish of you." Then her face softened slightly. "But it was also very noble and brave of you. You obviously care about my daughter a lot, and I *know* she cares about you. So . . . maybe her father and I were wrong about her not being ready to date. We're prepared to give her another chance at it, as long as it doesn't interfere with her schoolwork."

"It won't, I promise," Tom assured her. "She's the smartest person I know, and she'll make a great lawyer someday."

Mrs. Cox smiled again. "Well, she argued your case pretty strongly," she admitted. "I'd say that you're correct."

"And . . ." added Brittany, looking at her mother again. "The job?"

"Oh, yes." Mrs. Cox nodded. "I have a client who mentioned that he could use a pair of smart hands to help him out," she told Tom. "It's a decent part-time job for someone who knows a little science and is interested in learning some more."

Tom looked stunned. "Really? I'd *love* it!"

"Excellent." Mrs. Cox studied him appraisingly. "Perhaps you will work out, after all." She looked at her daughter. "I expect you home no later than eight, though."

"Right," Brittany agreed happily.

Mrs. Cox nodded at them all and then left them.

Tom hugged Brittany, still in a state of shock. "I can't believe how it all turned out so well," he admitted. "Even if I am still on probation as far as your parents are concerned. It's a lot better than I expected."

"Me too," agreed Brittany. She turned to Shelby. "Thank you, for everything. You proved Tom was innocent, and you gave me the will to go up against my parents. And win."

Shelby felt flattered and happy. "So, what say we go out and celebrate? Somewhere not too expensive?"

"Anywhere you like," Brittany said. "This one's my treat. I owe you all."

Noah rubbed his hands. "So, is it burgers or pizza?" he asked.

Hot Rock

So, eventually, I solved the case. Well, most of it, at any rate. I only missed out on a couple of clues. And I even helped true love win out in the end. So you can see why I love being a detective, can't you? And if you can't, just wait until I tell you all about my next case. . . .

About the Author

JOHN PEEL was born in Nottingham, England—home of Robin Hood. He moved to the United States in 1981 to get married and now lives on Long Island with his wife, Nan, their wire-haired fox terrier, Dashiell, and their feline terror, Amika. He has written more than sixty books, including novels based on the top British science fiction TV series, *Doctor Who,* and the top American science fiction TV series, *Star Trek.* He has written several supernatural thrillers for young adults that are published by Archway Paperbacks—*Talons, Shattered, Poison,* and *Maniac. Star Trek: Deep Space Nine: Prisoners of Peace* and *Field Trip* are available from Minstrel Books.

John has written several Nickelodeon titles for the *Are You Afraid of the Dark?* series and *The Secret World of Alex Mack* series.

GO BEYOND THE BOOKS AND ENTER THE WORLD OF

Bruce Coville's **MY TEACHER** is an **ALIEN**

CD-ROM GAME

You've always *suspected* that your *teacher* is an *alien*... But *no one* believed you. Now, to save your life, you have one week to *prove it*.

In this action-adventure CD-ROM game for fans of Bruce Coville's *My Teacher* book series, you'll encounter high-speed action sequences and mind-bending puzzles. You choose to play as one of the main characters—Susan, Peter, or Duncan—to help them foil the alien's evil plot. Your every move determines how the game will end—you'll have to think fast and act even faster to stop the alien before time runs out.

Available November 1997 **$34.95 Windows® 95 CD-ROM**

To order, call
1-888-793-9973

 Promo key: 440255 • Product number: 401174

http://www.byronpreiss.com

1369

#1 THE TALE OF THE SINISTER STATUES 52545-X/$3.99

#2 THE TALE OF CUTTER'S TREASURE 52729-0/$3.99

#3 THE TALE OF THE RESTLESS HOUSE 52547-6/$3.99

#4 THE TALE OF THE NIGHTLY NEIGHBORS 53445-9/$3.99

#5 THE TALE OF THE SECRET MIRROR 53671-0/$3.99

#6 THE TALE OF THE PHANTOM SCHOOL BUS 53672-9/$3.99

#7 THE TALE OF THE GHOST RIDERS 56252-5/$3.99

#8 THE TALE OF THE DEADLY DIARY 53673-7/$3.99

#9 THE TALE OF THE VIRTUAL NIGHTMARE 00080-2/$3.99

#10 THE TALE OF THE CURIOUS CAT 00081-0/$3.99

#11 THE TALE OF THE ZERO HERO 00357-7/$3.99

#12 THE TALE OF THE SHIMMERING SHELL 00392-5/$3.99

#13 THE TALE OF THE THREE WISHES 00358-5/$3.99

#14 THE TALE OF THE CAMPFIRE VAMPIRES 00908-7/$3.99

#15 THE TALE OF THE BAD-TEMPERED GHOST 01429-3/$3.99

A MINSTREL BOOK

Simon & Schuster Mail Order Dept. BWB
200 Old Tappan Rd., Old Tappan, N.J. 07675

Please send me the books I have checked above. I am enclosing $_____ (please add $0.75 to cover the postage and handling for each order. Please add appropriate sales tax). Send check or money order--no cash or C.O.D.'s please. Allow up to six weeks for delivery. For purchase over $10.00 you may use VISA: card number, expiration date and customer signature must be included.

Name _____

Address _____

City _____ State/Zip _____

VISA Card # _____ Exp.Date _____

Signature _____

1053-14

Have you ever wished
for the complete guide
to surviving your teenage years?

Your wish has just come true!

LET'S TALK ABOUT ME!

The Girl's Handbook for the 21st Century

Your Body
Your Personality
Your Future
Your Life

Being a teenage girl
has never been so much fun!

**A special handbook based
on the bestselling CD-ROM!**

COMING IN MID-SEPTEMBER 1997

An Archway Paperback
Published by Pocket Books

1384